CARIDES'S
FORGOTTEN
WIFE

CARIDES'S FORGOTTEN WIFE

BY

MAISEY YATES

MILLS
BOON

First published in Great Britain 2016
By Mills & Boon, an imprint of HarperCollins*Publishers*
1 London Bridge Street, London, SE1 9GF

Large Print edition 2016

© 2016 Maisey Yates

ISBN: 978-0-263-26262-9

Our policy is to use papers that are natural, renewable and recyclable products and made from wood grown in sustainable forests. The logging and manufacturing processes conform to the legal environmental regulations of the country of origin.

Printed and bound in Great Britain
by CPI Antony Rowe, Chippenham, Wiltshire

To Megan Crane/Caitlin Crews.

For all the times we've sat around
talking about how wonderful it is to
write these stories, and everything else.

You make my writing and my life more sparkly.

PROLOGUE

ANOTHER BORING PARTY in a long succession of boring parties. That was Leon's predominant thought as he pulled away from the ostentatious hotel and out onto the narrow Italian streets.

The highlight of his evening had been the most disappointing portion, as well. Being rebuffed by Rocco Amari's fiancée. She had been beautiful. Exotic. With her long dark hair and honey-colored skin. Yes, she would have made a wonderful companion for his bed tonight. Sadly, she seemed to be very committed to Rocco. And he to her.

To each his own, he supposed. Frankly, Leon did not see the appeal in monogamy.

Life was a glorious buffet of debauchery. Why on earth would he seek to limit that?

Though he had walked away empty-handed, he had thoroughly enjoyed enraging his business rival. He could not deny that.

The other man was possessive in a way that Leon could see no point in being. But then, he had never had feelings so intense for a woman.

He turned onto a road that began to lead out of the city, heading toward the villa he was staying in during his time in Italy. It was a nice place. Rustic, well-appointed. He preferred places like that to a penthouse in the middle of a busy business district. A fact that was, perhaps, at odds with other aspects of his personality. But then, being a contradiction had never bothered him.

He owned several estates worldwide, though none were as important to him as his estate in Connecticut.

The thought of that house, of that place, turned his thoughts to his wife.

He would rather not think of Rose just now.

For some reason when he thought of her after just attempting to bring another woman into his bed, he felt a tug of unaccustomed guilt. For the past two years, Rose had often made him feel guilty.

There was no real reason, of course. They were married, it was true, but in name only. He allowed her to do as she liked, and he carried on as he liked.

Still, it was easy to picture those wide, luminous blue eyes and feel…

His focus snapped back to the road, to a pair of headlights heading in his direction.

There was no time to correct. No time to react at all. There was nothing but the impact.

And a clear image of Rose's blue eyes.

CHAPTER ONE

"HE IS STABLE for the moment," Dr. Castellano said.

Rose looked down at her husband, lying in his hospital bed, broken, bandages wrapped around his upper arm, down over his shoulder and across his chest. His lip was swollen, a cut looking angry and painful at the center, a dark bruise bleeding color on his cheekbone.

He looked… Well, he looked not at all like Leon Carides. Leon Carides was larger-than-life, a man so full of power and charisma he was undeniable. A man who commanded respect with his every movement, his every breath. A man who stopped women in their tracks and demanded their full attention and admiration.

A man she had been on the verge of divorcing. But you could hardly hand a man divorce papers while he was lying in bed with severe injuries.

"It's a miracle he survived," the doctor continued.

"Yes," she said, her voice hollow. As hollow as the rest of her. "A miracle."

Some small part of her—one that she immediately set out to squash—thought it would have been much more convenient for him to have died there on the side of the road. Then she wouldn't have to face any of this. Wouldn't have to deal with the state of their union. Or rather, the lack of union.

But she banished it. Quickly. She couldn't stand being married to him anymore, but that didn't mean she wanted him dead.

She swallowed hard. "Well, thank heaven for miracles. Large and small."

"Yes."

"Has he been awake at all?"

"No," the doctor said, his voice heavy. "He has not been conscious since we brought him in. The impact was intense, and his head injury is…serious. He shows brain activity, so we do have some hope. But you know, the longer someone stays unconscious…"

"Of course."

It had taken her about twenty hours to get to Italy from Connecticut, and Leon had been unconscious for all that time. But there were all kinds of stories of people waking up miraculously after years. Surely he still had hope after a mere few hours.

"If you have any other questions, don't hesitate to get in touch. A nurse will be by in the next fifteen minutes. But if you have need of anything, just text this number." The doctor handed her a card with a phone number on it. She imagined this was what it was like to get special treatment at the hospital. Of course Leon would get special treatment. He was a billionaire, one of the most successful businessmen in the world. Wealthy, and powerful. Which meant that these sorts of things—as difficult as they were—would always be easier for people like him.

She held the card close to her chest. "Thank you."

The doctor left, closing the door behind him. Leaving her standing there in the room with nothing but the sounds of machines surrounding her.

Panic started to rise in her chest as she continued to look at Leon's still form. He wasn't supposed to look like this. He wasn't supposed to be breakable.

Leon Carides had always been more of a god to her than a man. The sort of man she had built up into fantasy as a young girl. He was ten years older than her. And he had been her father's most trusted and prized protégé from the time Rose was eight years old. She could hardly remember a period of time when Leon hadn't been involved in her life.

Carefree. Easy with a smile. Always so kind. He had seen her. Truly. And had made her feel like she mattered.

Of course, all that changed when they got married.

But she wasn't going to think about their wedding now.

She didn't want to think about anything. She wanted to close her eyes and be back in the rose garden at her family estate. Wanted to be surrounded by the soft, fragrant summer breeze, held in it as though it was a pair of arms, protecting her from all of this. But that was just a daydream. Everything here was too stark, too white, too antiseptic to be a dream.

It was crushingly real, an assault on her senses.

She wondered if there had been anyone else in the car with him. If there were, they hadn't said. She also wondered if he had been drinking. Again, no one had said.

Another perk of wealth. People wanted to protect you so they might benefit later. But the why didn't matter, as long as the protection happened.

Leon groaned and her focus was wrenched back to the hospital bed. He shifted, moving his hand, and the lines to the IV and the cord link to the pulse monitor on his finger tugged hard.

"Be careful," she said, keeping her voice soft. "You're plugged into…" She looked around at all the equipment, all the bags of saline and antibiotics and whatever else was being pumped into his veins. "Well, you're plugged into everything. Don't…*unplug* anything."

She didn't know if he heard her. Didn't know if he understood. But then, he shifted, groaning again.

"Are you in pain?"

"I *am* pain," he said, his voice rough, tortured.

Relief flooded her, washing over her in a wave that left her dizzy. She hadn't realized just how affected she was until this moment. Just how terrified she was.

Just how much she cared.

This feeling was so at odds with that small, cold moment where she had wished he could go away completely.

Or maybe it wasn't. Maybe the two were more tightly connected than it first appeared.

Because as long as he was here, she would *always* feel too much. And if he were gone, at least the loss of him wouldn't be a choice she had to make.

"You probably need more pain medication."

Though looking at him, at the purple bruises marring his typically handsome features, she doubted that there was pain medication strong enough to make it all go away.

"Then get me some," he said, his voice hard.

Issuing commands already, which was very much in his character. Leon was never at a loss. Even when her father had died and she'd been lost in a haze of grief, he had stepped forward and taken care of everything.

He hadn't comforted her the way a husband should comfort a wife. He had never been a husband to her at all, not in the truest sense. But he'd still made sure she was taken care of. Had ensured that the funeral, the legalities of the will and everything else were executed to perfection.

It was why, in spite of everything, it had seemed right to stay for the past two years. And it was also why, though it meant losing everything, she'd decided she had to leave him, no matter the cost.

But leaving him now…that didn't seem right. He hadn't been a true husband, but he hadn't abandoned her when she'd needed him, either. How could she do any less?

"I will have to call a nurse." She picked her phone up and sent off a brief text to the doctor: He's awake.

Just typing the words sent a rush of relief through her that she didn't want to analyze.

His eyes opened, and he began to look around the room. "You aren't a nurse?"

"No," she said, her heart thundering hard. "I'm Rose."

He was probably still disoriented. After all,

this was Italy, and she was supposed to be at home in Connecticut. She was probably the last person he expected to see.

"Rose?"

"Yes," she said, starting to feel a little bit more alarmed. "I flew to Italy because of your accident."

"We are in Italy?" He only sounded more confused.

"Yes," she said. "Where did you think you were?"

He frowned, his dark eyebrows locking together. "I don't know."

"You were in Italy. Seeing to some business." And probably pleasure, knowing him, but she wasn't going to add that. "You were leaving a party and a car drifted into your lane and hit you head-on."

"That is what I feel like," he said, his voice rough. "As though I were hit head-on. Though I feel more like I was hit directly by the car. With nothing to buffer it."

"With how fast you drive I imagine you might as well have been."

He frowned. "We know each other."

She frowned. "Of course we do. I'm your wife."

* * *

I'm your wife.

Those words echoed in his head, but he couldn't make any sense of them. He didn't remember having a wife. But then, he didn't remember being in Italy. He wasn't entirely certain he remembered…anything. His name. Who he was. What he was. He couldn't remember any of it.

"You are my wife," he said, waiting for the feeling of blackness, the open space around this moment that seemed to take up his entire consciousness.

There was nothing. There was only her standing before him. This hospital room, this bright spot of the present, with nothing before or after it.

If he kept her talking, perhaps she could fill the rest in. Perhaps he could flood those dark places with light.

"Yes," she said. "We got married two years ago."

"Did we?" He tried to force the image of a wedding into his mind. He did know what a wedding looked like. Curious that he knew that and not his own name. But he did. And still, he could not imagine this woman in a wedding gown. She had light-colored hair—some might call it mousy—hanging limp around her shoulders. Her figure was slight, her eyes too blue, too wide for her face.

Blue eyes.

A flash of an image hit him hard. Too bright. Too clear. Her eyes. He had been thinking about *her* eyes just before… But that was all he could remember.

"Yes," he said, "you are my wife." He thought he would test out the words. He knew they were true. He couldn't remember, but he still knew they were true.

"Oh, good. You were starting to scare me," she said, her voice shaking.

"I'm lying here broken. And I'm only just now starting to scare you?" he asked.

"Well, the part where you weren't remembering me was a little bit extra scary."

"You are my wife," he repeated. "And I am…"

The silence filled every empty place in the room. Heavy and accusing.

"You don't remember," she said, horror dawning in her voice. "You don't remember me. You don't remember *you*."

He closed his eyes, pain bursting behind his legs as he shook his head. "I must. Because the alternative is crazy."

"Is it?"

"I think it is." He opened his eyes and looked at her again. "I remember you," he said. "I remember your eyes."

Something in her expression changed. Softened. Her pale pink lips parted, and a bit of color returned to her cheeks. Right now she almost looked pretty. He supposed his initial impression of her wasn't terribly fair. Since he was lying in a hospital bed and since she had probably been given the shock of her life when she had been told her husband had been in a very serious car accident.

She had said she'd flown to Italy. He didn't know from where. But she had traveled to see him. It was no wonder she looked pale, and drawn. And a bit plain.

"You remember my eyes?" she asked.

"It's the only thing," he said. "That makes

sense, doesn't it?" Because she was his wife. Why couldn't he remember his wife?

"I had better get the doctor."

"I'm fine."

"You don't remember *anything*. How can you be fine?"

"I'm not going to die," he said.

"Ten minutes ago the doctor was in here telling me you might never wake up. So forgive me if I feel a little bit cautious."

"I'm awake. I can only assume the memories will follow."

She nodded slowly. "Yes," she said. "You would think."

A heavy knock on the door punctuated the silence.

Rose walked quickly out of her husband's hospital room, her head spinning.

He didn't remember anything. Leon didn't remember *anything*.

Dr. Castellano stood in the hallway looking at her, his expression grim. "How is he, Mrs. Carides?"

"Ms. Tanner," she corrected. More out of habit

than anything else. "I never took my husband's name."

She'd never taken him to her bed—why would she take his last name?

"Ms. Tanner," he repeated. "Tell me what seems to be going on."

"He doesn't remember." She was starting to shake now, all of the shock, all of the terror catching up with her. "He doesn't remember me. He doesn't remember himself."

"Nothing?"

"Nothing. And I didn't know...I didn't know what to tell him. I didn't know if it was like waking a sleepwalker, or if I should tell him."

"Well, we will need to tell him who he is. But I'm going to need to consult a specialist. A psychologist. I don't often deal with cases of amnesia."

"This is not a soap opera. My husband doesn't have amnesia."

"He sustained very serious head trauma. It is not so far-fetched."

"Yes it is," she said, feeling desperate. "It is extremely far-fetched."

"I know you're worried, but take heart. He is

stable. He is awake. Very likely his memories will return. And soon, I would think."

"Do you have statistical evidence to support that?"

"As I said… I do not often deal in cases of amnesia. Very often a person will lose a portion of their memories following a traumatic head injury. Usually just sections. It's uncommon to lose everything, but not impossible."

"He's lost everything," she said.

"He's likely to regain it."

"These other people. These people who have lost portions of their memory that you've treated. How often do they regain them?"

"Sometimes they don't," he said, a heavy admission that seemed pulled from him.

"He may never remember," she said, feeling dazed. Feeling her life, her future, slipping out of her hands. "Anything."

"I would not focus on that possibility." Dr. Castellano took a breath. "We will monitor him here for as long as we can. I would imagine that he will do much better recovering at home, monitored by local physicians."

She nodded. That was one thing she and Leon

had in common. His business often kept him abroad, which for her nerves was for the best. But they both loved the Tanner House in Connecticut. It was her favorite thing she had left of her family. The old, almost palatial home, the sprawling green lawns and a private rose garden that her mother had planted in honor of her only child. It was her refuge.

She had always had the feeling it was the same for Leon.

Though they tended to keep to their own wings of the house. At the very least, he never brought women there. He had allowed her to keep it as her own. Had made it a kind of sanctuary for them both.

It was also a condition of their marriage. When her father had hastily commanded the union when his illness took a turn for the worse, the house and his company had been a pivotal point. If—before five years was up—he divorced her, he lost the company and the house. If she left him before the five-year term finished, she lost the house and everything in it that wasn't her personal possession.

Which meant losing her retreat. And the work

she'd been doing archiving the Tanner family history, which stretched all the way back to the Mayflower.

So only everything, really.

And she'd been ready to do it, willing to do it because she had to stop waiting for Leon to decide he wanted to be her husband in every possible way.

Except now here they were.

"Yes," she said, feeling determined in this at least. "He will want to be moved to Connecticut as quickly as possible."

"Then as soon as it is safe to move him, we will do so. I imagine he has private physicians that can care for his needs."

She thought of the doctors and nurses that had cared for her father toward the end of his life. "I have a great many wonderful contacts. I only regret that I have yet more work to give them."

"Of course. But so long as he is stable we should be able to move him to Connecticut soon."

She looked back toward the room, her heart pounding. "Okay. We will do that as quickly as possible."

Going back to Connecticut with Leon was *not* asking Leon for a divorce. It was not moving toward having separate lives. It was not finally ridding herself of the man who had haunted and obsessed her for most of her life.

But he *needed* her.

Why does that matter so much?

The image came, as it always did, of herself sitting in the rose garden on the grounds of her family home. She was wearing a frothy, ridiculous gown, tears streaming down her face. Her prom date had stood her up. Probably because going with her in the first place was only a joke.

She looked up, and Leon was there. He was wearing a suit, very likely because he had been planning on going out that night after meeting with her father. She swallowed hard, looking up to his handsome face. Dying a little bit inside when she realized he was witnessing her lowest moment.

"What's wrong, agape?*"*

"Nothing. Just… My prom plans didn't exactly work out."

He reached down, taking her hand in his, and lifted her off the ground.

She couldn't remember Leon tou *fore. His hand was so warm, his to* *it sent a shock of electricity througn* *he.*

"If someone has hurt you, give me his name, and I will ensure he is unrecognizable when I'm through with him."

She shook her head. "No, I don't need you or my father coming to my defense. I think that would only be worse."

He curled his fingers around her hand. "Would it?"

Her heart was pounding so hard now she could hardly hear anything over it. "Yes."

"Then if you will not let me do physical harm to the one who has hurt you, perhaps you will allow me to dance with you."

She was powerless to do anything but nod. He pulled her against his body, sweeping her into an easy dance step. She had never been very good at it. One of the many things she had never quite mastered. But he didn't seem to mind. And in his arms she didn't feel clumsy. In his arms, she felt like she could fly.

"It is not you, Rose."

What isn't?" she asked, her words harsh, strangled.

"It's this age. It is difficult. But people like you, people who are too soft, too rare for this sort of assimilation required in order to fit in at high school, will go on to excel. You will go much further than they ever will. This is only temporary. You will spend the rest of your life living brighter. Living more beautifully than they could possibly imagine."

His words had meant so much to her. Words she had held close to her chest. Words she had clung to when she had walked down the aisle toward him, thinking that perhaps this was what he had meant. That this would be the bright, beautiful living he had promised two years earlier.

Their marriage had been anything but bright. Far from soaring, she'd spent the past two years feeling as though her wings had been clipped. She had a difficult time reconciling the man he'd been then with the man she had married.

Still, that memory was so large, so beautiful in her mind, even with everything that had passed between them since, that she could not deny he deserved her help.

And once he was better, once he was nursed fully back to health, then she would take steps to moving on with her life.

"Just tell me what I need to do," she said.

CHAPTER TWO

HE STILL COULDN'T remember his name when he was wheeled out of the hospital in a wheelchair and physically moved into a van designed to accommodate his limitations. But he did know that all of this ate at his pride. He did not like to need the assistance of others. He did not like to be at a disadvantage. And yet here he was, completely dependent, his pride in shreds.

Strange how he had no memories and yet he still knew these things. Bone-deep.

He *knew* his name. He knew his name because it had been spoken around him, over his head, as his wife and various medical professionals made decisions for him. But that was different than *knowing* his name. Than recognizing it. He was unable to remember who he was, but he wasn't stupid. Still, that seemed to constitute a compromise that he could not be trusted to make his own decisions.

The drive to the airport was long, and painful, every dip in the road aggravating some injury or another. He was lucky to have less broken than he did. But he was still far too sore to walk on his own. He had a couple of broken ribs, but other than that it was mainly deep contusions. So he had been told. He knew his extensive list of injuries. Had done his very best to memorize them, just so there was something in his brain he knew. Something he knew about himself.

But it was a rather depressing list of facts, he had to admit.

Still, they were the only facts he had.

According to his doctor, there were basics that he would be told. But there were some things that were best allowed to return organically.

He hated that, too. Hated that he wasn't just dependent on others for physical care. But that he was dependent on them for knowledge.

Every single person in the exam room earlier today knew more about him than he did. His wife knew whole volumes more than he did, undoubtedly.

He looked at her profile, her stoic expression as

she looked out the window, watching the scenery go by.

"I know you very well," he said. He hoped that by saying it it would make it so.

He must. He must know what she looked like beneath her clothes. He had touched her. Kissed her. Countless times, he would imagine. Because they were young—reasonably so—and in love, he presumed.

"I'm not entirely certain of that," she said.

"Why wouldn't I?"

She blinked, looking startled. "Of course you do."

The startled expression, he realized, was her correcting herself. Realizing she had done something wrong.

"Now you are being dishonest with me," he said.

"I'm not. I'm just doing my best to follow the doctor's orders. I'm not sure what I'm allowed to say and what I'm not allowed to say."

"I don't know that it's detrimental either way."

"I don't want to put memories into your head that aren't there."

"Nothing is there at the moment. I'm a blank

slate. I imagine I could very easily become victimized by you."

Color flooded her cheeks. Angry color, he guessed. "I'm not going to do anything to you." She turned away from him, her gaze fixed out the window again.

"So you say. But I am at your mercy."

"Oh, and I am so very terrifying."

"You could be. For all I know, this could be an elaborate ruse. I appear to be a very rich man."

"How would you know?"

"I had a very nice private room, and an awful lot of attention from doctors."

"Perhaps it is because you are a special case," she said, her voice so brittle it reminded him of crystal.

"Oh, I have no doubt of that. There are certain things that I seem to know. That I feel, down deep in my bones. Other things you have told me, such as my name, I simply have to believe. But my importance, the fact that I am a special case, that I know."

"Amazing," she said, her tone arch. "Apparently nothing can beat your ego out of you, Leon. That is an amazing feat, I will bow to that."

"So I am an egotist in addition to being special? I must be very charming to live with."

She blinked slowly. "You often travel for work. I typically remain in Connecticut. I suppose we find we get on best that way."

He lifted a shoulder. "Nothing unremarkable about that. I doubt very many people are suited to cohabitation."

"Another thing you're very confident about?"

"Yes. I am confident." He knew that. He felt that. He turned his focus to his wife. "This has been very trying for you," he said, trying his best to eliminate some of the waxen quality in her face. He did not like seeing her like this. Which was strange, considering he couldn't remember what she was like on a daily basis. Still, he knew he did not like her being in distress.

"Nobody wants to hear that their husband may never regain his memory."

"I can imagine. No man wants to hear he may never regain his memory."

She took a deep breath and let it out slowly. "I'm sorry. This has nothing to do with how difficult it is for me. You're the one who's injured."

"That isn't true at all. Of course it matters if

this is difficult for you. We are one flesh, are we not, *agape*?" He leaned in slightly, her light floral scent teasing his nose and stimulating... nothing. At least nothing in terms of memory. He was a man, after all, so it did stir something in his gut, low and deep. She was enticing, if not traditionally beautiful. "And if we are one flesh," he continued, "then what affects me also affects you."

She shifted, delicate color blooming in her cheeks. "I suppose that is true."

They were silent the rest of the ride to the airport, silent until he was wheeled onto a plane. A private plane. He had no memory of this, either, so he imagined not remembering her scent wasn't any more remarkable.

Once they were settled in the opulent surroundings, he leaned back in his chair. "This is mine?"

Rose nodded. "At least I hope so. I would hate to abscond with the wrong private plane."

"Then we really would make headlines."

"And of course we don't want that," she said, her tone firm.

"Do we not? I would like a Scotch."

"Certainly not," she said, frowning. "You've had enough pain pills to knock out a large mammal."

"I *am* a large mammal. And I am not unconscious."

"A larger one. Adding alcohol to the mix is a bad idea." She sat down in the chair across from him. "We do not want it getting out in the press that you are having issues with your memory. I have called a couple of media outlets and let them know you are recovering nicely from what was a traumatic injury. But that you will be back to normal in no time."

"Efficient of you. Do you work in my company with me?"

She shook her head. "No. But I spent many years helping my father with various details. Particularly after my mother passed away. So I'm well familiar."

"Am I involved in the same business as your father was?"

Her expression became guarded. "I don't think we should talk about business. In fact, I know we shouldn't. That is something I discussed with your doctor."

"How very nice of you to leave me out of it."

"It's for your health and well-being," she said, her words stiff.

"As though I am a child and not a grown man."

"You may well know less than a child does, Leon."

"I know a great many things," he countered. "I do not need to be sheltered."

"You're also not in any condition to go to work. Which means you don't need to be troubled with the details of business."

"As I said earlier, I am at your mercy." His head was pounding, and he really could kill someone for a Scotch. He could not be entirely certain, but he felt as though he did not often go this long without having a drink. He found the experience unsettling. Or perhaps, he was simply unsettled because his entire mind was a vacant field, with nothing stretching as far as he could see.

"I don't intend to let you atrophy on me now, Leon. We have a bit too much of a history for that." Of course they did. They were married after all. "You should sleep. When you wake up we'll be in Connecticut. And it's entirely possible everything will seem a bit clearer."

When the town car pulled up to the Tanner house Leon expected…something. A rush of familiarity, a feeling that he might latch on to. Rose had said this place was very important to him. In fact, she had acted as though his being here would be key to his recovery, and he realized as they advanced on the large, palatial home that he had been expecting something of a miracle when it came into view.

There was no such miracle.

It was a beautiful home, comprised of brick, with ivy climbing up the sides, making it appear as though the earth was attempting to reclaim the space for its own. There were no other houses out here. There was nothing but a large building off to the side he assumed was quarters for the staff, or at least had been at one time. Otherwise, there were large sprawling lawns in a vibrant green, backed by thick dark woods that gave the impression this house was in another time and space entirely from the rest of the world.

It was a beautiful home. But none of the magic he had been hoping for was present.

"This is it," Rose said, her tone small, as though she had already sensed his disappointment.

How was it that she could know him so well, even as he now didn't know himself? It was as though she could see inside of him, see into things that he could not. She had done so on the flight, and then again once they had landed. Of course, none of it seemed to matter, as her sixth sense mostly involved realizing that he was craving alcohol, and then denying him the satisfaction.

"Yes," he said. "So it is."

"You don't remember it." She sounded crestfallen.

"No," he said, surveying the bricks and mortar yet again. Waiting for a feeling of homecoming to overtake him. Waiting for anything beyond this fuzzy, blank confusion.

"You have been coming here often for as long as I can remember," Rose said. "Ever since you first started working with my father. When you became his protégé."

"Is that how we met?"

She nodded wordlessly, the gesture slightly stilted. "You would always sit with him in his study, but I can't enlighten you as to the content of those meetings. I was not included. Which stands to reason since I was a child."

He wondered then how old she was. If she was much younger than him. She did seem young. But then, he had very little reference point for that since he wasn't entirely certain how old he was.

"How old are you?" he asked.

"I don't think that's relevant. Anyway, it isn't polite to ask a lady her age. Is that something you've forgotten?"

"No. Survival skills made sure that was instilled deep inside of me still. However, it seems relevant. If I was here having business meetings and you were a child then clearly there is an age gap between us."

"Something of one," she said, her tone airy, distant. "But it isn't important. Why don't we go inside and I can show you to your room."

Her words didn't strike him as odd until they were wandering through the grand foyer of the home, surrounded by enough marble and fine art to make any museum curator jealous.

"To *my* room?" he asked.

"Yes," she returned.

"We do not share a room?"

She cleared her throat, fidgeting slightly. "Well, for the purposes of your recovery it would be extremely impractical," she said, neatly side-stepping the question. That was something he noticed she did with frequency.

"You did not make it sound like there would be any changes in our living arrangements when you talked about showing me to my room."

"You're making assumptions."

"I am. Enlighten me as to the situation, Rose. My head hurts and I find that I am in a foul temper."

She let out an exasperated sigh. "This is a very traditional house. With an obscene amount of rooms, as I'm sure you guessed. It's very much existing in its own time. And, I suppose you could say our living arrangement exists in the same time. We both like our space."

"Are you saying we live like some outmoded royal couple?"

"Yes. As I said, you are often away. For business. That means I often live on my own. So I elected to retain my own space, and that suited you just fine."

The answer seemed wrong to him. The arrangement seemed wrong to him. Which was strange, because he knew the man he was. The man who possessed all of the memories, all of the past experiences, had clearly found it the right way to conduct his marriage. Who was he to argue with that superior version of himself in full possession of all of the facts?

Still, he wanted to. Because his wife had come to his side immediately when he had been injured. Because her blue eyes were the only thing he truly remembered.

"Will you be able to make it up the stairs?" she asked, looking at him with concern in her expression.

"None of my limbs are broken."

"Your ribs are."

He shifted, wincing. "Only a couple."

"Tell me if this is too taxing." She began to lead the way up the broad, curved staircase. The steps were carpeted in a rich dark red, the banisters made of oak, polished to a high-gloss sheen. Money, history and tradition oozed from the pores of this place. And he had a strange sense that he did not belong. That somehow all of this was not his birthright, in any sense of the word.

He looked at Rose, her delicate fingertips skimming along the banister, her long, elegant neck held straight, her nose tilted up slightly. She was a bit plain, it was true, but she was aristocratic. There was no denying it. She was fine-boned, and refined, each and every inch of her.

He had the feeling that her skin was like silk. Smooth, perfect and far too luxurious for any mere mortal man to aspire to.

Somehow, he had her. Somehow, he had this house.

And he could make none of it feel real. Everything seemed to exist on its own plane. As if it were a strange dream he'd had once long ago.

A dream he couldn't quite remember.

He paused, a sharp pain shooting up his side, somehow going straight up his neck and through his jaw, rendering him motionless. As if sensing his discomfort, Rose turned. "Are you okay?" she asked.

"I'm fine," he returned.

"You don't look fine."

"Pain is a very determined thing," he remarked, continuing to stand there frozen as he waited for the lingering effects to recede. "It doesn't like to stay at the site of the injury."

"I've never been seriously injured. So I don't really have any experience with that."

"I…I don't know if I ever have been before. But either way I don't remember it. So it feels remarkably like the first time."

That made him wonder what other things might feel like the first time, and judging by the suddenly healthy color in his wife's face, she was wondering the same thing.

Of course, with his ribs being what they were, that wouldn't be happening anytime soon.

It was a strange thought, the idea of going to bed with someone he didn't know. Except, he *did* know her. But he might be different with her now. He might not be able to be the lover she deserved, or the one she wanted.

"Can you keep going? Or do you need for me to figure out a way to fix you a room downstairs?"

"I'm fine," he said, welcoming the interruption of his thoughts.

Finally, they reach the top of the stairs and he continued to follow her down the long corridor that led to his bedroom. Though *bedroom* was a bit humble of a word for what was in actuality an entire suite of rooms.

There was a home office, an extremely large bathroom, a sitting area and a room that actually contained a bed. "Do you have something similar?"

She nodded in affirmation. "Yes."

"We really are quite a bit like a royal couple." It made no sense to him, and it also felt wrong. He felt…captivated by Rose. Drawn to her. He couldn't imagine agreeing to separate bedrooms.

But perhaps things were different when his head was full of other things. Right now, it was only filled with pain, and her.

She was preferable to the pain, no contest.

She tilted her head to the side. "I find it very strange. The things you know and the things you don't."

"So do I. In all honesty, I would rather forget my surface knowledge of world customs and reclaim what I know about myself. But no one has consulted me on this."

"I understand. I should leave you to rest."

He was exhausted. Which seemed ridiculous considering he had spent most of the flight sleeping. He felt like this was definitely out of the ordinary. Being this tired. Also, being this sober.

He definitely had some strong impressions about what felt normal and what didn't. But he still wasn't entirely certain he could believe them.

"It would probably be for the best," he said.

"I'm going to confirm arrangements with the doctor I have coming in to check on you. The nurse, as well."

"I'm not an invalid."

"You have a head injury. And while we're reasonably certain you aren't going to die in the night, this is definitely out of the ordinary."

He couldn't argue with that. "All right then," he conceded.

"I'll wake you up when it's time for dinner." And then she turned and walked out briskly. And it was only then that it struck him that she never made any moves toward touching him physically. No small gestures of comfort. She hadn't even behaved as though she was tempted to lean in and kiss him before walking out.

But he supposed he would have to unravel the mysteries of his own mind before he set out to unravel the mysteries of his marriage.

CHAPTER THREE

ROSE FELT LIKE she was losing her mind. Which, really wouldn't do since Leon had so clearly lost his.

"That isn't fair. He hasn't lost his mind, he's lost his memory," she said, scolding herself as she paced the empty study.

The past two days had been the most trying of her entire life. And all things considered, that was saying something. She had endured an awful lot in her life. From her mother dying when she was a young girl to the loss of her father when she was only twenty-one. Continually feeling as though she didn't fit in with her peers, because she was too quiet, too mousy to be of interest to anyone. Because she would rather spend her time in dusty libraries than at wild parties. Because if she was going to shop for anything it would probably be stationery or books rather than the latest fashions.

She had spent the past two years married to a man who hadn't touched her outside of their wedding day.

Yes, it was safe to say that Rose Tanner had not had it easy.

Still, watching a man like Leon go through something like this, seeing him so reduced… It was… It was awful. She wished very much that she didn't care quite so intensely. Even when she was angry with him, even when she talked herself into believing that she hated him, it didn't change the fact that he was the most vibrant, powerful, incredible man she had ever met.

Seeing him injured. Seeing him unsure. Seeing him as mortal… It was as though the last remaining safety net in her life had been pulled away. She had already lost her other pillars. Her mother. Her father. And now, she was losing Leon, too.

Sure, he hadn't exactly been a fantastic emotional support in the past few years, but he had been steady. Predictable, at least.

He could have died a couple of days ago, and he might never again be the man that he had been. Acknowledging that was devastating in a way she could never have anticipated.

"Get it together."

Her stern admonishment echoed off the walls, and she bit back the rising hysteria that was threatening to burst out of her.

She should do something. Go out to the garden and tend to the roses. Finish cataloging her father's extensive library. Instead, she sat on a dark green settee in front of the fireplace and allowed a wave of misery to wash over her.

She wanted so very much to be done with this. To be done with all of this sitting still and waiting for something better to become of her life, for something better to become of her marriage.

She wanted Tanner house. Of course she did. But she knew Leon wanted it, too. Ultimately, she had been willing to walk away from both if need be.

But she couldn't walk away from him now. She needed to see him well. And then with a clear conscience she could go. She could get on with her life.

And if he doesn't remember anything ever?

For one brief moment the temptation to lie to

him overtook her. To tell him that the two of them were madly in love. To tell him that he had married her because he couldn't keep his hands off of her, not because he wanted to inherit her father's business empire and the home that had become close to his heart.

Yes, for one moment she was tempted. She wouldn't be human if she wasn't. She had spent so many years fantasizing about what it would be like to have Leon want her. To have him look at her and see her as a woman.

She couldn't do it. It would be… Well, it would be disgusting, but more than that it would be the furthest thing from what she really wanted. She didn't want Leon to be her prisoner. That was basically what he was already.

Actually, you're his.

She couldn't really argue with that. She had agreed to marry him, and then she had basically been installed in this house and left to rattle around the vacant halls. Meanwhile, he had continued to live life as though he were a single man.

The entire world knew they were married. The entire world also knew that he was an incorrigible playboy. And nobody knew that she had been trapped in an agreement to stay married to him for five years in order to make his ownership of her father's company permanent, and for her to end up with the home in the event of a divorce.

That was the prenuptial agreement, dictated by her father before his death.

But she wasn't waiting anymore. He could have the company. He could have the house. She just wanted to be free.

She had come to the point where she'd known she had two choices. To sit down and talk to him on one of the rare occasions he came home, and let him know how badly she wanted to give their marriage a chance. To tell him how she felt. Or, to ask for a divorce.

She'd opted for a divorce. Because there was no good way for the other conversation to end. She would lay her heart out there for him to see, risk everything and get rejected.

She'd decided she'd rather skip a few steps.

"Is it nearly dinnertime?"

She turned toward the sound of the gruff, sleepy voice and her heart nearly evaporated, right along with her good intentions. He was wearing nothing more than a pair of black, low-slung pants. His chest was bare, and she ought to be concerned about his wounds. About the bandage over his shoulder, the dark purple bruises streaked along his torso. Instead, her eyes chose mostly to fixate on his muscles.

On his perfectly defined chest, on the muscles in his abs that were rippling with each indrawn breath.

"I think so," she said, well aware that she sounded a little bit like she was the one who had been hit over the head.

"I'm starving," he said, crossing his arms and leaning against the door frame. He was holding a gray T-shirt in his hand, but made no move to put it on. "This is the first time I've been hungry since the accident. It's quite nice. I don't suppose you'll allow me to have a drink yet?"

"Still medicated, Leon."

"I'm starting to think that I would sacrifice pain medication for a drink." He frowned. "Do I drink a lot?"

She tried to think of Leon's habits. She wasn't overly familiar with them, since they didn't spend all that much time together. But, come to think of it, he was rarely without a drink in his hand.

"A bit," she said, cautiously. "Though I'm not quite sure what you're getting at."

"I have been craving a drink ever since I woke up. I don't know if it's simply because I'm in a situation of extreme stress or if I potentially have a bit of a dependency."

"You go out a lot," she said. "And why don't you put your shirt on?"

She sounded a little more desperate than she would have liked, but if he found it out of the ordinary, he didn't show it.

She wasn't supposed to pile a lot of information on him. She really was supposed to wait until he questioned things. But she was finding it difficult. Part of her wanted to dump the truth on him and then leave him in the hands of a doctor or nurse.

But he had been there for her the night of prom. He had also been there for her when her father had died. And this was what her father would want for her to do. Because he'd cared about Leon. Leon had always been the son her father had never had. Oftentimes she had felt like she was competing for affection, though she knew her father had loved her, too.

Her father wouldn't want Leon abandoned right now.

And so she would stay.

And she would do her very best not to upset him.

"I can't," he said, standing there still, the shirt clutched tightly in his hand.

"What do you mean you can't?"

"I'm having trouble getting the shirt on. My ribs are too sore." He held his hand out slightly, the shirt still clutched in his fist. "Can you help me?"

All of the air rushed from her lungs, her heart beating a steady rhythm in her ears. "I—" She was supposed to be his wife. There should be nothing remarkable about the request. There was nothing remarkable about it either way. He was an injured man and he needed help. He didn't need her to be weird.

She cleared her throat and crossed the space between them, hesitating for a moment before she reached out and took hold of the shirt. Their fingers brushed as he relinquished it to her, and a shiver ran down her spine.

She needed to get a grip.

"When you say I go out a lot, you mean that I go to parties?"

She nodded, swallowing hard, her throat suddenly dry. "Yes." She held the shirt so it was facing the right direction and gathered the material up. "You need to…duck your head or bend as much as you can."

He bent slightly and she pushed the shirt over his head, dragging it down to his shoulders, his skin scorching hers as her knuckles brushed against his collarbone.

"And you?" he asked.

She looked up at him, her eyes clashing with his. He was so close. So close that it would be easy to stretch up on her toes and close the space between them. She'd only kissed him once. At their wedding in front of a church full of people.

What would happen if she did it again?

She blinked, trying to shake off the drugged feeling that was stealing over her. "Lift your arm as much as you can," she murmured.

He complied, his fingers grazing his bicep as

he slipped into the shirt. "Do you go out with me?" he pressed.

She wasn't sure how to respond to that. She wasn't supposed to be dumping information on him, and beyond that, she didn't really want to. "I prefer to stay at home."

She pulled the shirt down the rest of the way over his torso, her knuckles brushing against the crisp hair and hard muscle as she did, a hollow sensation carving itself into the pit of her stomach.

It brought to mind all manner of things she'd scarcely allowed herself to fantasize about. Possibilities she'd only just now let go, as she'd accepted the fact her marriage had to end.

And now this. This unique and particular torture that brought her closer to her fantasy than ever before, and further away at the same time.

She took a step away from him, hoping to catch her breath.

He frowned, straightening. "I go out without you?"

He looked just as sexy with the shirt on. Tight and fitted over his muscular frame. She blinked and looked away.

"Sometimes." She looked up at the clock and saw that it was nearing six, which meant that dinner would be ready. She felt absolutely rescued by that. Maybe when they had a whole table between them she'd be able to breathe again. "I think it's time for us to go and eat," she said. "I'll show you the way to the dining room."

"You have a full staff here?" he asked, as they made their way through the house.

"Yes. I have kept everyone on since my father died. I didn't see the point in changing anything." She cleared her throat. "More than that, I guess I have desperately tried to keep everything the same."

"We both love this house," he said. "It's something we share. At least, you have told me I love this house."

"Yes, you do. And so do I. I was very happy here growing up. It is the only place I have memories of my mother. I remember hiding up at the top of the staircase and looking down, watching their massive holiday parties. My mother was always the most beautiful woman in the room. She looked so happy with my father. I wanted...

I wanted more than anything to grow up and have that be my life."

Her throat tightened and she found herself unexpectedly blinking back tears.

"Is that not our life?" he asked.

He sounded… He sounded hopeful. It was a very strange thing. Typically, Leon spoke with an air of practiced cynicism. He was not the sort of man who held out hope for much of anything. He was grounded. A realist. It was why she cherished the very few soft moments she had ever had with him. Because when he took the time to be caring she knew that he meant it.

But when it came to things like this, flights of fancy, romantic ideas about life and adulthood, she didn't expect him to care at all. Much less be able to envision himself as part of it.

She found that she wanted to lie to him. Or, if not lie, be a bit creative with the truth.

"This house is ours. To do with it as we wish. You have been very busy since my father's death. Fully establishing yourself as the head of the company, expanding. We have not yet had time to throw any large holiday parties."

"But we intend to?"

"Yes," she said. That really wasn't strictly true. She imagined that he never intended to. And she'd been planning on leaving him before next Christmas anyway.

Though she had wished... She had hoped, once upon a time.

Recently, she had given up on it. She didn't even imagine her own future in this house, much less a shared future. But there was no benefit in telling him that now.

When they walked into the dining room the table was already beautifully appointed. She had warned the staff to keep a low profile. The doctor had told her that it was best to keep things as low-key as possible for Leon while he recovered. It was easy to focus only on the amnesia, which was of course the thing that both of them were most aware of, and forget that he also possessed quite a few physical injuries.

"They made your favorite," she said, sitting down in front of the steak and risotto that had been prepared for them. There was red wine at her seat. Water at Leon's.

"This seems a bit cruel and unusual," he said, eyeing her drink.

"I don't need to drink it."

"And that," he said, his tone hard, "seems remarkably wasteful. You can drink wine. I cannot. One of us should."

"Awfully giving of you."

"I feel that I am generous."

She couldn't help herself. She laughed. "Do you?" She lifted her wine to her lips and took a sip, suddenly grateful for the extra fortification that it would provide.

"Yes. Are you contradicting me?"

"Of course not," she said, looking down at her dinner. "You give to a great many charities."

"There you have it," he said, picking up his knife and fork. "Incontrovertible evidence that I am in fact generous."

"Perhaps," she said, slicing her steak slowly, "there is more than one type of generosity."

His dark eyebrows shot upward. "Is that so?"

She lifted one shoulder. "Perhaps."

"Do not speak in code. That is hardly less strenuous on my brain."

"I am not supposed to bombard you. Much less with my opinions. Opinions are not fact. You need facts."

"It is your *opinion* that I am not generous. At least not in every way."

She let out a long breath, feeling frustrated with herself. Feeling frustrated with him. With the world. She wanted to get up out of her chair, throw her cloth napkin on the floor and run out onto one of the grand lawns. Then perhaps she might rend her garment for dramatic effect and shout at the unfeeling sky.

Of course, she would do none of that. She never did.

Instead, she looked up at him and spoke in an even, moderated tone. "Of course you are."

"Now you are placating me."

She let out an exasperated sigh. "Are you trying to start a fight?"

"Don't be silly. We never fight."

"How could you possibly know that?" she asked, a strange sensation settling in the pit of her stomach.

Of course, he wasn't wrong. They had never fought. She had done nothing but idolize him for most of her life, and then she had married him. And in the two years since they had gotten married they'd had so little interaction they hadn't been able to fight. And, frankly, probably wouldn't have even if she had seen him every day.

He was indifferent to her, but he'd never been cruel. There had never been enough passion between them for there to be a fight.

"I just do," he said.

"You are so arrogant. Even now."

"Stingy and arrogant. That is your opinion of me. How is it that we never fight?"

"Perhaps because you are not often around," she said, taking her first bite of steak and making a bit of a show about chewing it so that he would perhaps cease his endless questions.

Leon looked across the table at his wife. He did not know quite how to read the exchange that had just taken place between them. She was irritated with him, that much he was certain of. He wondered how often that was the case. He wondered if this was unusual, if the stress of the situation was simply overtaking her, or if she didn't usually show him her irritation.

Or, more troubling, if he didn't typically notice it.

She had made several comments now about him frequently being away. She made him sound as though he was an absentee husband at best. Her childhood dream centered around her home being filled with parties. Centered around her hosting these events with her husband, to recapture a part of her life that was clearly past.

Both of her parents were gone. She had made no mention of any siblings. He appeared to be all that she had left, and yet he had seen no evidence that he did very much at all to support her emotionally.

That bothered him. Regardless of whether or not it bothered the man he had been before the accident was irrelevant to him in the moment. She was caring for him. And she clearly felt uncared for in many ways.

He felt compelled to remedy that. If he had to sit around this manor and do nothing but heal for the next several weeks he might as well focus on healing his marriage as well as his body.

It was deeper than that, too. Deeper than just a desire to right a wrong from the past.

Rose was his only touchstone. She was the only person who knew him. The only person he really knew. She was his anchor in an angry sea. And without her, he would be swept away completely.

He needed to shore up the connection between them.

He had lost himself. He could remember nothing of who he was. And from the sounds of things, their connection was much more tentative than it should be.

She was all he had. He could not lose her.

There was only one solution. He had to seduce his wife.

CHAPTER FOUR

IT HAD BEEN nearly a week since Leon's return to the manor and he still hadn't remembered anything. Rose was fighting against restlessness, hopelessness and the growing tenderness in her heart whenever she was around him.

As if that tenderness is anything new.

True. She had always felt…something for him. More than she should. He didn't care for her like that. He never had. But she could never quite stamp out that…that *hope*. That need. For someone who had been confronted with so much loss she retained rather more than a normal amount of idealism.

There was some part of her that believed steadfastly in happy endings. And being rewarded for good behavior. That was probably why she had always done exactly as her father asked. Why she had done her best to wait for Leon to come around to the idea of being her husband.

And why she had never actually sat down and told him how she felt. Better to close the door herself than have him do it.

"Don't start hoping again now. Once he remembers...everything will go back to the way it was."

She lay down on her back on her favorite settee, staring at the ornate ceiling. Then she heard heavy footsteps on the marble floors. She sat up, clutching the book she had been reading to her chest.

"Rose?" Leon strode into the room, looking much more alert and able than he had only a few days ago. He had been resting quite a bit, and had taken several meals in his room since that first night here. It seemed to have paid off.

"Just reading," she said.

"What are you reading?"

"Nora Roberts."

"I don't think I've read her. Maybe I have. I wouldn't know."

She laughed in spite of herself. "I doubt it."

"It's not the sort of thing I would usually read?"

"Unless it's business-related literature you don't strike me as the sort of man who reads."

"You don't think?"

"You're usually very confident about who you are, and how you see yourself. What do you think?"

"I think that…I cannot imagine myself going to university. But that's impossible. Being in the position that I'm in I must have gone."

"You didn't," she said, imagining that it was all right to confirm this.

But you don't think it's okay to confirm that your marriage is not quite what it seems?

She gritted her teeth and banished that thought. One thing at a time. And anyway, she intended to have this discussion with him. She intended to end their marriage. But she doubted news of a divorce would be overly welcome to him right now. Especially not when they needed to keep his condition a secret. Especially not when he would have no one else looking out for him. No one else who knew him to help him through all of this.

"Then how… I know enough to know that that is not typically how the world works." He rubbed his hand over his chin, his skin scrap-

ing against the whiskers there. The sound was…
strangely erotic.

Rose had no experience with men. Not intimate experience. Beyond that single chaste kiss
on their wedding day, and the strangely arous-
ing experience of putting his T-shirt on him,
she hadn't really had any physical contact with
a man. Why would she? She had been waiting
for Leon. Fool that she was.

As a result, she imagined she was a bit more
affected by everyday things than a woman with
greater experience would be. Looking at the situation with a little bit of distance she felt sorry
for herself. Poor, innocent Rose quivering over
whiskers.

Too bad she had no distance in the situation.
She had…longing that she could do nothing
about, sadness that never seemed to go away,
that permeated her entire being and settled a
heaviness over her chest, and a deep fear that
Leon would never remember anything. Coupled
with an almost equally deep fear that he would
remember everything and she would have to
leave this house, leave him, and move forward

with her goal of independence. Of letting go of her feelings for him.

"I'm fuzzy on the details, and I'm sorry about that," she said, trying to ignore the heat in her cheeks. "All I know is that you were working for my father, for his company. In a very low-level position. You were a teenager. You had not graduated from school. Instead, you left and went straight into the workforce. You did something at the company to catch my father's eye, and from there he began to mentor you. He took a very personal interest in you, and he began to groom you to be his protégé."

"My family wasn't rich," he said, a strange, hollow look taking over his eyes. "I know that. I'm from Greece. We were very poor. I came here by myself."

It struck her then, how little she knew about him. She knew he was Greek, that much was obvious, but she didn't know about his background, not really. She was struck then how little she knew him at all.

He had appeared in her life one day like a vapor and she had hero-worshipped him from that moment on.

That is, until she had fully realized that he would never quite conform to the fantasy she had built around him in her mind. She didn't wonder why he had married her. The perks of the union were obvious. Her father had been dying, and he wanted to see her settled. He had offered the company and the estate as incentives to Leon, and had put a time frame on the union likely to make sure the two of them gave it an adequate enough try.

All of that made sense. But she suddenly realized that she was the one who didn't make sense. What had she been hoping for? What on earth had she possibly thought would come from all of this? Who did she imagine he was? That was the problem. *All* of it was imaginary.

As she sat here in the library attempting to reconstruct who Leon was for his own sake, she realized just how much of the puzzle she was missing.

It made her feel… It made her feel small. Selfish. As if she had only ever seen him as an object of fantasy, who lived and breathed to serve her girlish dreams.

"Are you all right?" he asked.

She blinked. "Yes. Do I not look all right?"

"You look as though you have been hit across the face with a mackerel."

She tried to laugh. "Sorry. It's just…I don't actually know as much about you as I should. When confronted with the gaps in your memory I'm forced to examine the missing pieces of my knowledge."

He frowned. "I suppose I bear some part of the blame in that. If not most of it."

"I don't think that's true. I think in this case the fault is squarely mine."

"I cannot help you with it now. I don't have answers to any of the questions."

"I don't expect you to," she said, feeling rather weak and pale.

"I do know a few things," he said, squaring his shoulders, his eyes taking on a determined glitter. That made her feel more at ease. That reminded her of the Leon she had always known.

Sharp, determined, ever in command.

"That's reassuring," she said.

"I know that we are having dinner outside on the terrace tonight. And I know that it's going to be Maine lobster. Which I know is your favorite."

"How exactly do you know that? You didn't know what *your* favorite was only a few days ago."

It wasn't really because of his memory loss that she found this strange. She wasn't sure he had ever known her favorite foods.

"I am fully capable of making inquiries. Probably better than I was just a week ago. My entire life has become dependent on answers, and in part, the quality of my questions. I did my best to rustle up some members of the staff so that I could figure some things out about you."

"You didn't have to do that." She felt slightly panicky. As though she was being given a gift that was entirely unearned.

"I know I didn't. But you are my wife. Not only that, you have been taking care of me ever since the accident."

"Not entirely. We've had a nurse on call. The doctor has been in constantly. I—"

"Just knowing you were here has been invaluable." He smiled and she felt it all the way down, deep. It made her stomach tighten, made her heart flutter. Why was it always like this?

He extended his hand, his dark eyes meeting hers. She looked down at it as though it were a poisonous snake.

"I'm leading you to lobster. Not to your doom," he said.

She hesitated, feeling very much like she didn't deserve to touch him. Feeling very much like this was intended for a woman who didn't exist. The devoted wife she wasn't. The devoted wife she would be if Leon had any interest in being a husband in real life.

Or she was overthinking it. This was just dinner. This was only his hand.

She took a deep breath and wrapped her fingers around his. Lightning shot over the surface of her skin, crackling over her entire body, leaving her breathless, leaving her knees weak. She hadn't touched him since the wedding. She hadn't touched any man since then. She wasn't entirely certain she had *really* touched anyone at all.

Her father was gone. And even when he'd been here, he'd been spare on physical affection. All of her close friends, the ones she'd made in her two years of university while starting her history degree, had moved away. None of them were spending their twenties rotting in their parents' estates. They had all moved to Manhattan, London, exciting places. They were all pursuing careers, or higher education. Bigger goals than clinging to good memories. They were out making *new* memories. And until this moment, until his skin touched hers, she didn't realize how incredibly lonely she had become.

She had no one to blame but herself.

And this is why you're leaving.

She took a deep breath, trying to do her best to keep her reaction to him concealed. But then she made a terrible mistake. She looked up, her eyes meeting his, and what she saw there astonished her.

His eyes weren't blank. They weren't flat. They were… They were molten. The heat there a perfect reflection of the fire that was rioting through her core.

"Come on," he said, his voice rough.

She could do nothing but follow him. Which

was terribly telling. Not just of this moment, but of the past fifteen years or so.

And once they were outside, her breath caught in her throat, all of the sensations building in her chest, making it impossible for her to do anything but stand there and tremble. He was touching her. And right before them was a beautifully appointed table set for two, a candle at the center.

It was like something that had been torn from her fantasies. Her girlish fantasies. When loving him had simply meant aspirations of sweet romance, holding hands and making sophisticated conversation.

Back before she had realized that there was much more to the connection between men and women than candlelight and hand-holding.

"Is something wrong?"

She looked at him, at his fierce expression. There was an intensity behind his eyes that she couldn't decode. All she knew was that she had waited most of her life to have him look at her like this. And for some reason he was looking at her this way now. She was… She was powerless to resist. Utterly and completely held captive by that look in his eyes.

"Nothing's wrong," she lied, making her way across the expansive terrace and taking her seat at the table.

She noticed then that Leon had a glass of water in front of his plate rather than wine. "I didn't think you were on pain medication anymore," she said.

"I'm not. But as I'm not entirely certain what my relationship is to alcohol I decided it best to continue to abstain. I seem to have done all right without it in the past week. Why start now?"

She nodded slowly. The truth was, Leon overindulged in everything. It was difficult to say what specifically he might have a problem with, and what specifically he just chose to indulge in to excess. But she was grateful that he was choosing to remain completely sober tonight. The idea of him being drunk and amnesiac made her feel far too much like the predator he had implied she might be when they had first left for the airport in Italy.

"Oh. Well. Maybe I should drink something else then."

"You're fine. It occurs to me that we've been talking rather a lot about me. I want to hear more about you, Rose. Because it isn't only myself that I have forgotten about. I don't remember anything about you."

Her heart was thundering hard, her throat suddenly dry. "I'm not sure that I'm a very interesting topic of conversation."

"I doubt there is anything more interesting to a man than the topic of his wife."

"We don't… We don't have that sort of relationship," she said, the truth stumbling out of her mouth uneasily.

"Why not?"

"I'm not sure that you are well suited to marriage."

He frowned. "Have I been unkind to you in some way?"

"No," she said, trying to dispel his fears quickly. She was afraid that he was imagining himself to be some kind of monster when that couldn't be further from the truth. "You are independent. We do not live in each other's pockets, as you have already noticed by virtue of the fact that we have separate bedrooms. We do not often take long meals together out on the terrace. We do not often share our innermost thoughts."

"Why did you marry me?" The words were so confused, so utterly filled with disbelief. It was shocking. To hear him question why on earth she might have married him.

"I could give any number of reasons a woman would marry you. You are incredibly handsome. Successful. And as for me…I am… Well, let's not be dishonest about the situation, Leon. I am quite plain."

He frowned even more deeply. Then he reached across the table, the edge of his thumb touching the corner of her mouth. Her heart slammed hard into her breastbone, her entire body going rigid, every fiber of her being on high alert to see what might happen next. He traced the line of her upper lip, then dipped down to the lower one before sweeping his thumb up to her cheekbone, dragging it slowly across her skin.

"I will confess that my first thought was that you were plain. But as I have spent time with you, as you have cared for me…I can no longer see what I first did. The only real memory I have, the only concrete image in my mind is your eyes. You are what I *remember*, while everything else is vague impressions and hazy ideas. If it is not entirely absent altogether. Your eyes are my truth, Rose. How could I find them, or you, anything but incredibly beautiful?"

She had stopped breathing now. Any moment, she had a feeling she was going to tip sideways in her chair and lose consciousness completely. But to have him look at her like this, to have him say those things… This entire nightmare was being twisted into a dream. Perversely, she was enjoying it. Perversely, it was everything she had ever wanted. But not like this.

Still, she found she couldn't turn away. "That is… It is an incredibly nice thing to say."

"I'm stingy and arrogant, remember? I am neither generous nor particularly nice, to hear you tell it. I am not being kind when I say these words. I am being truthful. There's a limit to the sorts of truths you can tell in my position. There are very few things I know for certain. But this is one of them."

He shifted the position of his hand, cupping her face, his palm warming her. Igniting her.

"You are my wife. I wish to know everything about you."

He dropped his hand away from her face, drawing it back to his side of the table. She cleared her throat nervously, shifting the cutlery on the table in front of her as a displacement activity.

"Did you go to university?" he asked.

"Yes," she said.

"What did you study?"

She shifted, feeling uncomfortable and edgy beneath his intense dark gaze. "I was a history major. As you've probably guessed, I like old things. Really, the older and dustier the better."

"Is that a jab at my age?"

She laughed. "Um. It wasn't, but that's an interesting point. No, I like the smell of books, musty pages and such. Aged velvet furniture that's always a little damp."

"Doesn't sound too appealing to me."

"No. Of course not. Your room here is all modernized."

"I like things sans dust and mold, what can I say," he returned. "So you did your history degree."

"No," she said. "I went for two years. And then I stopped."

"Why?"

"I married you."

Her answer settled uncomfortably between them. An accusation, when she hadn't meant it to be one.

"Which begs the question," he said, "that I have been dying for the answer to. How old are you?"

She fiddled even more intensely with the silverware. "Twenty-three."

"So you were twenty-one when we married."

"Twenty. I was just shy of my birthday, and we have been married a little over two years."

"That seems a bit too young."

She lifted her shoulder. "My father was dying. We both knew it. Knowing that I was safe with you, knowing that we were settled brought him a lot of joy. Neither of us wanted to deny him that."

"And then your father died and…I have been off partying. I left you here in this house by yourself with no finished degree doing…"

"You helped. When he died. You didn't just abandon me and go to parties. You supported me. You took care of so many details when I was far too emotional to do it myself."

The relief on his face touched something deep inside of her. "Well, that's something."

"And I've been organizing my family history. Our family tree, which stems back to the founding of the country, actually. So it's very rich and…you know, complicated."

"Wonderful. So I left you here to grow moldy with the old furniture you love so much. How generous of me."

"No," she said, her chest tight. Because it was the truth. Her father had died and Leon had returned to the exact lifestyle he had been living before their marriage. He had never touched her, not once, but he had continued to sleep with other women. She knew it. She wasn't blind. Gossip magazines were alight with it. The poor, sad Tanner heiress and her wandering husband. But she didn't want to tell him that. She didn't want to tell this man that.

How strange that she did not want to disappoint him with the truth about himself.

"You are not being truthful with me."

"I'm not entirely certain the truth is beneficial in this situation."

He rose from his seat and came to stand in front of her before dropping to his knees. They were eye level, and he was so close she could smell the soap on his skin, could feel the warmth coming off his body. She was seized by the desire to touch him. To close the distance between them. But she didn't. She just sat there, frozen as ever.

It turned out she didn't have to close the distance, because he was the one to do it. He reached up, cupping her cheeks with both of his hands, drawing her face down toward him. "Then we shall make a new truth. I see no reason why we cannot make a new life. You have shared with me your dreams, and I find that I like the sound of them."

"You aren't working right now. You are… housebound. I am the only entertainment you have."

His dark gaze turned stormy. "You make me sound like a child."

In some ways, he was. In some ways, he always had been. A man with a very short attention span who was constantly on to the next toy. The newest thing, the shiniest thing. As a girl she had found it exciting. His flashy cars, his sharp wardrobe, even the beautiful women he would sometimes bring to her father's parties. Until the sharp claws of jealousy had sunk deep inside her. Until she had wanted to occupy the position those women were in.

It was the moments in between that got her. That held her affection for him. The spare times when she'd caught a hint of haunted darkness around the edges of his bright smile. The times when he'd looked at her and seen down deep.

The times he'd looked at her, period, and not just past her.

"I..."

"I am not a child," he said, his voice a dark temptation she couldn't turn away from.

And before she could say another word, before she could protest, before she could even breathe, Leon had closed the distance between them. And he was kissing her like she had never been kissed before. As he had never kissed her before, since he was the only man she had ever kissed.

His lips were hot, firm and commanding as they moved over her own, his tongue a slick, sweet enticement as it delved deep inside her mouth, sliding against her own. Immediately, her breasts felt heavy, her core a hollow ache, wet with need for him at the first touch of his mouth to hers.

She was drowning. In this. In him. In the desire. Completely and utterly at its mercy.

She wasn't even sure she cared. Because she was being swept away on a tide that she couldn't even hope to fight against. Desire dictating her every response, her every movement.

She felt… She felt ravenous for him. Completely and totally starved of the one thing she had craved for so long. She wrapped her arms around his neck, leaning out of her chair and crushing her breasts to his chest, nearly sighing with relief as she pressed herself against him. She wanted to meld herself to him completely, wanted to get lost in this forever.

It was a sickness, a kind of madness that overtook her completely. The desire to feel his skin against hers, to have nothing at all between them. His memories didn't matter. His broken ribs didn't matter. His betrayal of their vows didn't matter. All of the hurt, all of the torture she had endured over it didn't matter.

Nothing mattered but this. The fact that she was kissing him finally.

He slid his hand down her back, pressing her more firmly against him. She parted her thighs, resting the part of herself that was aching the most for his touch up against his hardened arousal.

He growled, drawing his hand down lower to cup her rear, pressing her even more tightly to him, rolling his hips against hers.

It occurred to her then that it wasn't only alcohol he had gone a long time without. Granted, she had gone twenty-three years without this kind of sexual contact, but Leon was accustomed to more.

And it was that thought that found her pulling away from him, running her shaking hands through her hair and sitting back in her chair. "I'm sorry," she said, the words rushed.

He looked at her, frowning. "Why are you sorry?"

"You don't remember anything. You don't remember us. And you're injured…"

"This," he said, his eyes meeting hers meaningfully, "has nothing to do with memory. This is another bit of honesty, I think."

Except it wasn't. Because they didn't do things like this. Because he had never touched her before. She couldn't bring herself to voice that admission. Could not do that to what was left of her pride.

"I think it would be for the best if we held off on things like this."

"Why is that?" he asked. "Is it because you are so angry with me about something that happened before?"

"It's because I don't feel right about asking you to sleep with a stranger." It was nearly the truth.

"Everyone is a stranger to me. I'm a stranger to myself. And yet I seem to sleep in my own body every night."

"It's different. And you know it."

"Is it?"

"I think you're just…just male. And therefore would come up with any excuse for sex."

He shook his head slowly, his dark eyes searching. "You are my wife. You are not a stranger to me. And I can feel…that there is something broken between us. I know it, as surely as I know certain things about myself. I do not need a memory to know that I wish to fix that."

Her throat tightened, pressure building in her chest. "It is not entirely on you to fix it."

"I want to try."

She gritted her teeth, trying to hold her emotions in check. "Let's wait. Let's wait until you remember." The words nearly choked her, because the last thing she wanted was to wait. If they waited, he would remember his indifference. If they waited, he wouldn't want to fix what was broken. Because in Leon's eyes their marriage wasn't broken. Why would it be?

With their current arrangement he was allowed to behave as he saw fit. To do exactly what he wanted whenever he wanted with whomever he wanted. Once he remembered that their arrangement consisted of her staying home while he behaved like a man with no wife at all he wouldn't want to change a thing.

"You are not my doctor, *agape*."

"No, I'm not. But I am the one who—"

"Don't make the mistake of thinking that because I don't have my memories I'm not in full control of my desires. A man does not need a memory to know that he wants a woman. He feels that in his body. In his blood. Mine burns for you. My mind may not remember, but my body suffers no such affliction."

She drew in a deep, shuddering breath, the weight of all the restraint, of the denial pressing down on her. He was promising things that didn't exist outside of misty fantasy for her. Pleasure, satisfaction on a level she could hardly comprehend. But it wasn't for her. Not really. And she had to resist. No matter how enticing it was.

"No," she said, standing from her chair and sweeping past him, not pausing to look back at him as she walked straight into the house. She kept going. She nearly ran. All the way through the house, up the stairs, down the corridor and into her bedroom. She shut the door tightly behind her, and leaned back up against the wall.

And she couldn't help but feel she had run away from her salvation.

CHAPTER FIVE

SHE WAS BREATHING HARD, her heart fluttering in her chest like a trapped bird in a cage.

She wanted him. And this sorely tested her. All of her willpower, all of her restraint. He was offering her what she wanted on a platter. Seemingly. But she knew that as decadent, as wonderful as it all seemed, it would be poison in the end.

"It would be. It would kill me." She spoke those words aloud into the emptiness of the room. Trying to make herself believe them. Trying to force herself to feel it.

She squeezed her eyes shut tight, curling her fingers into fists. And she waited until she stopped shaking before she moved away from the wall.

When she could catch her breath she reached around and took hold of the tab on the zipper, drawing it down, feeling as though she was casting some of the weight off as she let her dress fall from her body and pool at her feet on the floor. She wandered into the bathroom, turning the tub taps on and letting the water run until it was hot.

She unclipped her bra, flinging it onto the floor, not caring where it landed. She pushed her panties down her thighs, leaving them behind, too. Then she walked back into her bedroom, digging through her closet until she found a pair of sweats, something that would entice her to stay away from Leon for the rest of the night. If she put on anything too silky, anything that might not humiliate her to stand before him in, she could not guarantee that she wouldn't go and find him later.

With that thought in mind she stared down at the pair of pajama pants in her hand, then shoved them back in the drawer, digging until she found a slightly older, slightly baggier pair. Insurance. It was what she needed.

Additional insurance came in the form of large white cotton panties that would provide more than full coverage, and handle any Leon incidentals that might occur.

She grabbed hold of an equally ancient sweat-shirt and added it to her pile of clothing before heading back into the bathroom.

She wasn't foolish enough to think she would behave rationally now she'd tasted him. Wars were started over sex. The desire for it. The anger over someone else having it in a way you didn't like. Or with someone you wish you were having it with.

Sex was powerful. And she knew better than to think she was immune.

The water was hot, steam beginning to fill the air. She took a deep breath, sighing as she exhaled. Then she turned toward the counter and began to pin her hair up, slowly, methodically, trying to erase the past few moments from her mind.

"I wonder." She heard a rich, masculine voice coming from behind her and she turned. There was Leon, standing in the door, his dark eyes like black fire. "I wonder how many times I have stood here in this very place and watched you prepare for your bath like this. I have no recollection. This does not make my mind itch in any way."

Heat scorched her skin, fascination and embarrassment warring for equal place inside of her. He had never seen her naked before. No man ever had. But of course, he didn't know that. Of course, he wouldn't have any concept of just what an invasion this was.

That was her own doing. There was no one to blame for that but herself. And she still wasn't doing anything to correct it.

"An itch in your mind?" She looked around, desperately searching for a towel, something, *anything* to cover her exposed body.

"That is what it feels like sometimes. When something is familiar but I can't grab hold of it. As though I have an itch deep in my brain that I can't quite get to. But this… This is free of all of that. Perhaps because when I look at you it becomes difficult to think at all."

She swallowed hard. And she forgot to look for a towel. Forgot to be embarrassed. She was completely frozen in her tracks. It would be easy—or it should be—to move her hands strategically and offer herself some modesty. But she felt like she'd been turned into a pillar of salt. Punished for looking at him when she should have turned away.

You don't want to cover yourself. You want him to keep looking at you.

Yes, she did. As disturbing a realization as that was, she did.

Historically, people were very stupid when it came to sex. She was proving beyond a doubt that she was doomed to repeat history.

"You do say very nice things," she said, her voice thin, soft.

"Have I always?"

She shook her head. "You don't say unkind things. But…"

He took a step into the bathroom and her entire body stiffened. "But I do not lavish you with the sort of praise you deserve. I get that sense. I get the feeling that I never adequately appreciated how glorious a sight you were." He was gazing at her openly, with no shame at all. Like this was the Garden of Eden and nudity was simply right.

"Do you even remember what women look like naked? Perhaps that's all this is. Perhaps there is a strange amount of novelty that you're contending with here." She still hadn't managed to move at all. She was standing there, completely bare, her heart pounding hard, her limbs trembling. She felt like a frightened squirrel staring down a large predator she had no hope of escaping.

You don't even want to escape. You want to offer him your neck.

She gritted her teeth, squeezing her knees tightly together, trying to tamp down the restless feeling that was growing between her thighs.

"I *do* remember what women look like naked. Oddly enough. Not one specific woman, but it is not as mysterious to me as you might think." He took another step toward her, then another. "I know that you think we should wait. But I want you to listen to me. I feel very much like what we had before this was broken. I said that to you downstairs, and I still mean it. I don't care what happened. I don't care where we were. I have a sense that you and I are the right thing. You are the woman I want. The woman I married. Whenever I lost sight of it, why I lost sight of it, it doesn't matter. If you can forgive me then I want to move forward as husband and wife. And I want to be husband and wife in every sense of the word." His voice got lower, grew rougher. "And I don't want to wait for my ribs to heal. I don't want to wait for a memory that may never come back. My life is a blank, barren field, Rose. I have…I have nothing. I have nothing but this connection to you, this need for you. Give me this. Give me something other than emptiness."

What he was offering her was a dream come true. All of her girlish fantasies come to life. It was what she had hoped would happen after their wedding two years ago. That wedding night that never actually eventuated.

Two years a wife, and she was still a virgin. Pining after a man who had held her heart as long as she could remember. It was enough to make her want to cry just thinking about it. Enough to make her want to curl up in a ball and wail for just how sorrowful a situation it was. She had wanted him for as long as she could remember, and she had been denied him. She had married him. And she had never once pushed. Not for anything. Even when she had decided that she would divorce him she had immediately rushed to his side the moment she had heard about his injury. Because what else could she do? Leon held all of her heart. There was no denying that.

It was why she had to divorce him even at the expense of the house if she wanted to retain her sanity. Because as long as she lived in hope she would never move on with her life.

And here he was, standing there, offering her hope. Offering her everything she had ever wanted to hear.

She just wasn't strong enough to say no. She had been strong, for so long, in so many ways. She had done her best to be strong for her father when her mother had died, even if he had done his best to hold it all together for her.

She had stayed strong in the face of his illness, in the face of his impending death. She had stayed strong even as he had asked her to marry Leon, so that he would know that she was protected. Even while the very thought of entering into a loveless union with the man who held every last piece of her soul killed her by inches.

She could not sacrifice anymore. Not for one more moment.

Leon was offering to make this marriage work.

He wanted her to be his wife in every way. How could she deny him?

How could she deny herself?

This time, she was the one who took a step forward. Moving toward him. Her heart was in her throat, pounding, making her feel light-headed, dizzy. But even so, she took another step toward him, and then another.

He was the one who closed the distance. He was the one who ran out of patience. He wrapped his arm around her waist, pulling her tightly up against his body, a feral growl on his lips. She could feel him. All of him. His heat, his hardness, the intense thrust of his arousal up against her hip.

Oh, how she wanted him. There were no words for the depth of her desire. For the depth of her longing, her need.

It wove itself around her body, like the vines that overtook the Tanner house, creeping ever higher until it threatened to consume her. Need wrapped itself around her throat, made it impossible for her to breathe. Impossible for her to think.

"Are you afraid of me, Rose?" His voice was

so soft, so tender and so full of concern, it made her own heart ache in response.

"Of course not."

"You look at me as though I am a monster of some kind."

"Not you. This thing between us. All of this. It feels like a monster. Like something that could consume us both."

He laughed, the sound rusty, hard. "Yes, I agree." He dragged his thumb along her cheekbone, his gaze filled with wonder. "Has it always been like this?"

"For me," she said, the word strangled. "For me it has always been like this."

"I think it has been for me, too."

She laughed. "You can't possibly know that."

"Of course I can. Just as I know I am generous."

"I already told you we have differing opinions on that."

"Which leads me to believe that I perhaps demonstrate the things I feel differently than people might usually. But it doesn't mean I don't feel them. This is an old feeling, Rose. I know it is. It's as much a part of me as my blood.

There's nothing foreign about it. Nothing unusual. It simply is. And much like any other part of myself I'm not sure that you could remove it without destroying me completely."

"You don't say things like this," she said, feeling almost desperate to pull away now. This was too much. Because this wasn't him. Not really. This was not the kind but distant man she had always known.

The Leon that she knew did not feel this for her. If he did, he would have touched her a long time ago. If he did, he wouldn't spend his nights in bed with other women.

But she couldn't say any of that. Not in this moment. Not now. And she couldn't pull away, either. Because no matter how strong the compulsion was, it could not begin to compete with the desire to stay in his arms.

"Let's not talk," she said. "Please, kiss me."

He didn't hesitate. He lowered his head, closing the distance between them. And she ignited. All of the need, all of the desire she had felt out on the terrace was magnified now. Magnified by the feel of his large hands spanning her bare waist, of her nipples pressing against the rough fabric of his shirt. Magnified by the fact that she was utterly and completely enslaved to him now. The fact that she was not trying to fight it anymore, even for a moment.

If this was a war, she was conquered.

This was wrong. But she didn't care. She was doing the wrong thing. And she was doing it for herself. She had spent a great many years trying to do the right thing. And she had gotten nothing in return.

She wasn't afraid of being wrong. She didn't even feel guilty. She simply felt exhilaration. Freedom. Here she was in the arms of the man she had always wanted, and she would think of nothing else.

She had always imagined that the moment Leon touched her he would know that she loved him. That she would betray every part of herself if he so much as swept his hand over her cheek. But this was different. So different than how she had ever envisioned it. Because he assumed that she loved him. He also assumed that he loved her.

But because of that…there were no secrets to keep. This was no revelation for him. And there was nothing inside of herself to protect. It made her feel strong. It made her feel not quite so vulnerable.

It made her feel not so much like the neglected virgin bride she'd been.

She pressed her hands against his chest, reveling in the feel of him, in the hardness of his muscles, the evidence of his strength. Before she could think it through, before she could stop herself, she was working the buttons on his shirt, separating the fabric, brushing her fingertips over his bare skin.

She had been struck by his beauty the day he had walked into the library without a shirt. And now she was touching him.

Her fingers shook as she pressed them against his skin, as she traced the definition of his muscles, his coarse chest hair abrading her fingertips as she continued to explore him. He was everything a man should be. But then, of course he was. Her desire for men was shaped around him. Her needs had never been generic. Her need had always been for him. Always and only.

He held the back of her head with his hand, deepening the kiss, his tongue delving deep as he tasted her slowly, leisurely. His other hand slid low to cover her bottom, his fingers pressing deep into her flesh. It was a possessive hold. It was not a hold of a man who was unsure of what he wanted. He wanted her.

It didn't matter what he had wanted in the past. This was now. And he was choosing her.

She squeezed her eyes shut tight, pouring everything into the kiss.

She didn't know what she was doing. She had no practical skill in the art of seduction. She had nothing more than her passion. And she doubted there was a woman alive who felt as passionately about Leon Carides as she did. She doubted there was a woman alive who felt this passionately about any man. This was nearly fifteen years in the making for her. And what she lacked in practical skill she more than made up for in desire.

She pushed his shirt off his shoulders, marveling at the way he was constructed. She doubted there was a man alive so perfectly formed. At least, there was no other man alive so perfectly created for her. She kept her eyes squeezed tight, did so in order to keep the tears from falling.

Nerves, emotions, threatened to strangle her. This was desire like she'd never known existed. In the abstract, wanting him was something she could control.

Late at night in her bed, when she imagined being with him, when she imagined him touching her skin, she dictated the movements. She controlled how fast things went, how quickly she brought herself to completion.

In reality, she controlled nothing of what he did. And her need was a blazing wildfire, burning out of control. It was terrifying. Exhilarating. Intoxicating. It was so much more than she had ever imagined it could be.

But it was moving far faster than she had anticipated. The hand that had been resting on her bottom had now dipped down between her thighs, teasing her slick folds, ramping up her need until she could hardly breathe. If he moved his hand just a little bit higher, he would push her over the edge completely. With nothing more than a simple touch, a simple kiss, she knew that she would lose her control.

And so what if she did? She was past the point of caring. In fact, she embraced it. This was what she wanted. Wild. Beyond desire. Beyond shame.

It was as though everything between them had been burned to the ground. As though they had been given a chance to start again. No one else was given this chance. They were. This was for them. This was for her. This was her chance to make a new memory of herself. Even if he did remember everything in the past, he would remember this, too.

In this moment, she could create a new image for herself. He would finally see her as a woman, because he could no longer remember her as that plain, bookish girl she'd been.

If it was that that stood between them, if it was his affection for her father, whatever it was, that was lost here. Obliterated. Gone.

There was nothing but Leon. Nothing but Rose. Nothing but the need that was sparking between them, hot and out of control.

He growled, sliding his hand down to her thigh, hooking her leg up over his hip, then the other, bringing the damp part of her up against the hardness of his arousal, sending a streak of pleasure through her body. She gasped, and he began to carry her out of the room, carry her toward the bed.

"The bath," she said, feeling dazed.

"I suppose we don't want to cause a flood," he said, depositing her at the center of the mattress and abandoning her as he went to turn the water off.

She had a moment to rethink then. A moment to gather her thoughts. A moment to flee.

She stayed where she was.

He appeared a moment later, filling the doorway, his broad shoulders, heavily muscled chest and narrow waist so utterly masculine, so completely captivating, it stole her breath.

And then there was the hard press of his erection against the front of his jeans. The absolute and complete evidence that he truly did want her.

She bit her lip, nerves threatening to swamp her.

"There's that look again," he said, his tone gentle. "Please don't be afraid of me, *agape*." He came to stand beside the bed, his hands on the snap of his jeans. "I only want to make you feel good. I want to make this a memory we share. I want…I want you to feel close to me."

She tried to speak. She tried to say that she wanted that, too. But she already did feel closer to him than she ever had. But she couldn't form the words. She couldn't make her voice work. Couldn't force anything through the tightness of her throat.

"Sometimes I wonder if you have lost your memory, as well," he said, undoing his jeans then drawing the zipper down slowly.

Her heart nearly stopped. "I haven't. It's just that… You're different. This is different."

"I am sorry." He pushed his jeans down his narrow hips, exposing his rigid arousal. He was so beautiful. So rampantly masculine. So…large.

"For what?" She managed to scrape the words past her dry throat.

"For the way I was."

He joined her on the bed then, closing the distance between them, drawing her naked body up against the length of his. His erection was hard, so very hot against her skin. It was unfamiliar. It was wonderful. He ran his hands over her curves, warm, large, soothing. She found that she wasn't as nervous now.

She just wanted. She was filled with a restless,

overpowering ache that was threatening to un-ravel her completely. If she didn't have more of him. More of this.

"What do you like?" he asked, his voice a rich, deep whisper that whisked along her veins.

"You," she said, the deepest and starkest truth there was.

"Surely you must like something specific."

"Everything you do. Everything you are. That's what I want. It's all I've ever wanted." The admission poured from deep inside of her. From deep within her soul. And she couldn't be embarrassed.

"You are too easy on me, I think. I think you should perhaps make me grovel. I think you should perhaps make me beg." He leaned in, pressing a hot openmouthed kiss to her neck.

"I'm the one that's about to beg," she said, her voice breathless.

"There's no need. I am at your mercy," he said, "your willing slave." He kissed a line down her neck, down to the curve of her breast, his breath hot across her sensitized nipples. Then he traced the outline of one tightened bud with his tongue before sucking her in deep. She gasped, arching up off of the bed, sensation shooting through her like an arrow, hitting its target unerringly.

"You are very sensitive," he said, his voice rough. A smile curved his lips. "And do not ask how I know you are particularly. I simply do."

She had not been about to ask him anything, if only because she felt as though her voice could no longer form words. Her brain certainly couldn't muster up the amount of cells required to say anything. Indeed, sentence formation was beyond her. He had transformed her, transformed her into a creature of *feeling* and *needing*. Who could do nothing but simply wait for the next sensation to bombard her.

Still, she managed to speak. "This has only made your arrogance worse, I hope you know."

"I am a terrible trial to you," he said, a smile curving his lips. "I can see. But I feel you enjoy my arrogance."

He transferred his attention to her other breast, repeating the motion that he had done with the first, sending another direct shot of pleasure straight through her system. She shifted, parting her legs, rubbing herself against his thigh, seeking some kind of release from the pressure that was building inside her.

"So impatient," he said.

"I am," she panted. "If you could kindly move a little bit faster."

"I only have this one chance to make a memory of our first time again. If I never get my memories back this is all I will have. I intend to take my time."

He licked and kissed his way down the tender skin of her stomach, moving to the vulnerable flesh on her inner thigh before sweeping his tongue right through her slick folds. She cried out, sensation racking her body, wave after wave of release shuddering through her. And when it was over, she was panting, shaking and ready for more. Ready for everything.

"Leon," she said, feeling desperate. "I need you."

"I'm not finished," he said, lapping at her again, his fingers teasing the entrance to her body.

"I want to explore you," she said. "I want… Everything you did to me I want to do to you."

She wanted to taste every masculine inch of

him. To glory over the way he was made. To revel in a fantasy long awaited. Come to scorching life finally, at long last.

"No. It is my turn."

And before she could protest he worked a finger deep inside her, continuing to tease her with his wicked tongue as he did. This sensation, the penetration was new for her. She loved it. Loved the feel of having him inside her. He added a second finger, stretching her gently as he continued to tease her clitoris with his tongue.

He couldn't know that she needed this. That she needed this introduction, this moment of preparation. And yet somehow he seemed to sense it.

Pleasure built all over again, and she found herself close to the edge once more. Needing him. Needing all of him.

"Not enough," she said, panting.

"You want me inside of you?" he asked, his voice slurred as though he had finally had that drink he'd been craving for more than a week. As though she were the alcohol that he had so long desired. As though he was drunk on her, on her body. On desire.

"Yes," she said.

He rose up, positioning himself between her thighs, kissing her lips deeply as he tested the entrance to her body with the blunt head of his arousal. She braced herself, tensing her muscles involuntarily as he thrust all the way home. Pain lanced her, sharp and unexpected. She had known it might hurt a bit, but this was more than a little pain. But then, Leon was more than just a bit of man.

She clung to his shoulders, her fingernails digging into his skin as she tried to catch her breath. He just stared at her, his dark eyes inscrutable, unreadable. He flexed his hips, and she feared that he would pull away. Instead, he pushed back inside of her, groaning as he did.

And then they were lost. In need. In this intense, primal desire that had overtaken them both.

Pain was forgotten. Nerves were forgotten. Everything was forgotten but her desperate bid for completion. She ran her fingertips over his back, down to his strong muscled butt, back up again, sweeping over the square line of his jaw, the deep grooves around his mouth. She tilted her head to the side and kissed his neck, scraped her teeth along the tendon that was held so tight, that betrayed just how desperately he was clinging to his control. Just how close he was to losing his grip.

She could feel his muscles begin to tremble, could feel him growing closer to the edge. His own loss of control snapped hers. She cried out, arching against him, a deeper, more profound orgasm rocking her as her internal muscles tightened around him.

He thrust twice more. Hard, intense, a growl on his lips as he found his own release, holding her tightly against his body when it was all finished.

She was dazed. Storm-tossed. Completely and utterly at the mercy of what had just taken place between them. She could hardly remember her own name. And for one hysterical moment she imagined that was how Leon must feel. Wiped clean. Fresh. Remade.

There were worse things than being remade with him.

"Your ribs," she said, suddenly remembering that he was injured. She moved her hand to touch his side and he caught hold of her, his dark eyes clearer now, his expression intense.

"Tell me," he said, not moving from his position on top of her, his fingers like iron around her wrist. "How is it that my wife of two years was still a virgin?"

CHAPTER SIX

HIS WIFE WAS a virgin. There was absolutely no question about it. At least, she had been up until a few moments ago. What he didn't know was *why*.

She was beautiful, and he was incredibly attracted to her. More than that, he had married her. It made no sense at all. Although he supposed it didn't make any less sense than any other part of this situation they found themselves in.

A sense of cold dread filled his stomach and he turned toward her, his heart pounding hard. "Did you not want me? Did I force myself on you just now?"

"You know you didn't. I said that I wanted you."

"Then how is it we had never consummated our union?"

Rose looked as though she was going to curl

in on herself. She moved away from him, sliding beneath the edge of the blankets, disappearing completely beneath them. "You were the one who didn't want me."

"How is that possible?"

"I don't suppose it matters how it's possible. Only that it is. And even knowing that, I said yes to you while you couldn't remember how little you wanted me. In real life—whatever you want to call it—Leon Carides does not want Rose Tanner. You didn't know that. I did." She reappeared, her face peeking out from beneath the blankets. "I'm sorry."

It took him a moment to process the words. It was taking him time to process all of this. "You are my wife."

"You keep saying that like it means anything, but believe me, Leon, it has meant *nothing* to you over the past two years."

"I want it to." He didn't know where the certainty came from, but he felt it all the same. Bone-deep and as real as anything. He had no memory, that was true. And it meant he counted on these feelings. They were all he had.

"You might not. You might not when you remember why you didn't in the first place."

"Why didn't I?"

"I don't know," she said miserably.

"Start from the beginning. Why did we get married?"

"For the house. This house. For the company you run now. And for my father. He was dying, and you were like a son to him. He loved you, Leon. And he wanted all of this to be yours. I think... I think it brought him a lot of joy to know that you would be the one taking care of me. There was no one in the entire world that he trusted the way that he trusted you."

Leon's stomach tightened. Because to hear Rose tell it her father had trusted him, had cared for him. And he had done...what with that? He had married his daughter as a formality. And then had... Rose had said much about how he often went out. The thought made him feel sick.

"Rose," he said, his tone grave. "When I go out what is it that I do?"

She didn't answer immediately, her expression mutinous. "You like to drink."

"What else?" he asked, his voice scraping his throat raw.

"You like… You like women."

Pain lanced his chest, his brain, his ribs. Everything. "I have been unfaithful to you."

"We don't have a conventional marriage. As you can see now you have never touched me. Not before this. You kissed me on our wedding day and that was it. And you told me… You told me that it didn't have to change anything. I think the offer stood for myself, as well. I think you expected I might go out and find a lover. But you are my husband, Leon, and I couldn't—"

Of course she couldn't. Rose was too sweet. So young, so innocent. He was older, harder. And he had no idea why he was the way he was. All he knew was that with everything a blank slate inside of him, without the built-in excuses, without the baggage, he was disgusted with himself.

He had been given this gift. This woman. This wife. And he had treated her with nothing but neglect.

"I want to do better," he said finally.

"What?"

"I want to do better for you. Better for us. We

have a chance to change things, to make a new start." He shook his head then, his words tasting wrong in his mouth. "I suppose I have that chance. You remember everything. You know exactly who I am. You know exactly what I've done to you. And it seems the simplest thing in the world to ask for forgiveness when you can't remember your sins. I don't deserve it."

"Leon, I should've told you from the beginning about our marriage. But… It didn't seem…" She was blinking back tears now, and he hated that he was making her cry. He had a feeling he had done so more than once. "I think I didn't want you to know because I was hoping this would happen. But that was manipulative of me."

"I'm not angry. Not at you. I married you to get this house, to get your father's company and to placate him, and what did you get?"

"Well, if we divorced after five years, I got the house." She swallowed. "But I imagine you would have wanted us to stay married so that everything would stay with you, too. Marriage is different when you aren't exactly living as a married couple. I think for you that's never been an issue."

"It is an issue to me now. And I'm not angry with you. How old am I, Rose?"

"Thirty-three," she said.

"Ten years older than you."

"That doesn't—"

"And answer me this—when you married me what did you expect would happen?"

Color flooded her cheeks and she turned away from him. "Well, frankly, I imagined that something much like tonight might happen on our wedding night."

"So I did not tell you that I intended to live my life as a single man until after you had already made vows to me."

"Yes," she said.

"Then I feel you have only been trying to claim what you rightfully are owed. And I think that we need to try and fix this. Together."

"What about when you remember? What about when things… What about when they go back to the way they were?"

"I won't lose *these* memories just because I gain the old ones. I can't imagine anything on earth changing what is between us now." He reached out, brushing his thumb over her cheek, over her impossibly soft skin. "How can I ever go back to living in the same space as you without wanting to touch you all the time? How could I possibly return to other women's beds when yours is the only one I want to be in?"

And then he leaned in and kissed her, and they did not speak for the rest of the night.

Leon appreciated the fact that his doctor had ordered him to sit out in the sun a few hours a day so he didn't end up with vitamin deficiencies, but he would much rather be in the house than sitting out on the terrace.

In the house with Rose, naked in his arms as he brought her pleasure again and again.

He was insatiable for his wife. For this woman he'd never touched before his accident. A woman he'd married and left a virgin.

He frowned. He could not understand why he'd done that. And the questions… It was concerning. Because at this point he could not imagine holding her at a distance. He wanted to hold her right up against him, skin to skin, at all times.

He was obsessed with her.

He looked out at the view of the lush grounds of

the estate. He had this home. He had Rose. And yet he was never here. He had never touched her.

Instead he had gone out and slept with other women.

The idea sent a lash of shame streaking through him like the crack of a whip. Hot. Painful. But somewhere beneath the self-loathing was…concern.

Why? Why hadn't he touched her? Why had he held himself back?

"How are you feeling?"

He turned in his seat and saw Rose standing in the doorway, wearing a flowing dress with a flower pattern, teasing him with just a peek of long slender leg.

It was easy to push his questions and concerns to the back of his mind when he could see her. As soon as he saw her he wanted to push her dress up past her hips and bury his face between her thighs.

It was preferable to thinking.

"Well," he said. "I can dress myself now anyway."

A wicked light danced in her blue eyes. "I would rather undress you."

Heat flared in his gut and he pushed his previous concerns down even further. "I am glad you think that way, *agape*."

She stepped out onto the terrace and he began to push himself into a standing position, a dull pain shooting through his midsection as he disturbed his injuries.

"Don't," she said, holding her hand out. "Just sit. There's plenty of time for...touching later."

He frowned. "I want to touch you now."

She extended her hand and he gripped her slender fingers in his, a flash of lightning hitting him low and hard. "How's that?"

"Not enough." Never enough. How would it ever be enough? He might never have all the answers to who he was. But he had her. She was his beacon. His touchstone.

She smiled and it moved places inside of him. It hurt. As though heat was touching ice for the first time.

"Leon..."

"Why history?" he asked.

"What?" she asked, blinking.

"What made you decide to major in history?" If he couldn't strip her naked, he would convince her to reveal herself in other ways. She was all he had. She filled his brain, his body, his soul. There was nothing else, and he wasn't even certain he cared.

Why should he make an effort to know himself, in all his filthy, broken lack of glory, when he could know her?

"Well, I like research," she said. "And if you research the past you can accomplish a lot of it in…silence. Reading. Exploring the basements and attics of old houses and libraries."

"You like to be alone?"

She frowned. "I like time to think. And… questioning texts is much…safer than questioning actual people."

He had a feeling she applied that to more than just history.

"Is that why you never said anything to me?" he asked. "About my behavior?"

She looked away from him, her pale throat contracting as she swallowed hard. "We married for the company and for the house. It never seemed…"

"That is not the only reason," he said, his voice growing rough. "I know it wasn't."

He could not have been blind to his attraction to her. And his attraction wasn't new. He was confident in that.

"It was as far as I knew," she said, her tone stiff. "For you anyway." She softened on that last part, and it made his chest ache.

He did not deserve her. He was certain of few things but that was one of them. "I do not think that's the case."

But there was something. Something that had held him back from her. Something that had kept her a virgin, and kept him away as often as possible.

Part of him wanted to know.

Most of him simply wanted things to stay as they were. Because here and now, he had her. He never wanted to let her go.

Everything went perfectly over the next few weeks. And if Rose felt a small amount of disquiet, ever present and ominous, resting in her chest, she did her best to ignore it. Leon was… He was the most caring, solicitous man she had ever known. And the sex… Well, that was much better than anything she had ever imagined she might experience. It was incredible. He was incredible. There was so much passion between them it was impossible to imagine things had ever been cold.

She felt like a newlywed. After two years.

It was a strange experience, one that made her feel like she was floating through her days. She wasn't unhappy about it. Not in the least.

Perhaps a little bit uneasy, though.

She pushed that thought down and continued on through the halls. She was looking for Leon, who had become more mobile and was beginning to wander about the estate more. He still didn't remember anything, but he was feeling much better, and he had taken it upon himself to relearn every inch of the grounds.

She imagined he was somewhere in the gardens.

This isn't real. When he remembers he's going to go back to the way he was. When he remembers, he'll be consumed with work, with desire for women who actually know what they're doing. Not sad virgins who have spent most of their lives cosseted away.

She gritted her teeth, ignoring that mean little

voice. It was the source of her disquiet. And it was, unfortunately, far too accurate for her to deny.

"Ms. Tanner." The housekeeper rushed to where Rose was standing, a worried look on her face. "Someone is here to see Mr. Carides."

Rose shook her head. "That's impossible. Leon can't see anyone. We don't want anyone to know about his memory."

"It's just… It is a woman."

Rose's stomach dropped into her feet. "Is it?"

As far as she knew Leon didn't have mistresses in a traditional sense. He slept with other women, that was true, but there were none that he had a special connection with.

"A woman. A lawyer. And a baby."

Rose didn't even respond. Before she could think anything through she was running straight toward the front door, her heart pounding so hard she could scarcely breathe.

She was half expecting her housekeeper to have made everything up. For there to be no one standing at the door. For it to be empty, and everything to be the way that it was a few moments ago. Perfect, and beautiful, and not falling down around her.

The woman was beautiful. Blonde, tall, expertly made up. She was dressed simply, but effectively, every piece of clothing accentuating her coloring, her shape, and highlighting her beauty. The man next to her was grim-faced, clad in a sharp suit. And right in front of them was a car seat, the shade drawn over the part where the baby sat, concealing it from view.

"I am Leon Carides's wife," Rose said, her voice trembling. "What exactly is happening here?"

"My client has some things to discuss with Mr. Carides." It was the lawyer who spoke, the woman beside him extremely silent and pale.

"I don't know if you heard or not, but my husband was recently in a serious car accident. He's still recovering."

"Still, I imagine he will want to hear what we have to say," the lawyer said.

"I want to hear what you have to say," she said, her tone insistent.

"If you can get hold of him, and ask his permission to hear the details, I'm certain we can fill you in."

"I don't see any point in being coy about it," the woman said, crossing her arms beneath her breasts, her expression turning determined. "I want to see Leon. I want to give him his baby."

She had known what this was. The moment she'd heard who was at the door she'd known. But she still didn't want to believe it. Didn't want to believe what this woman was saying.

"I'm sorry," Rose said, asking for clarity she didn't truly need. "What?"

"His baby," she said. "The child is his, and it's time for him to take responsibility."

By the time they were all seated in Leon's office, Rose was in a daze. Leon did not look like he was faring much better. He could only stare blank-faced at the woman who was claiming to be the mother of his child. A child who was only four months old.

Rose bit back a cry of hysteria at the thought. Yes, she knew he had been with other women over the course of their marriage. But never, *ever* had she been asked to deal with the reality of it in quite such a tangible way.

The baby hadn't made a sound since arriving—it was like a little doll, sitting in the bucket seat. A girl, with a pink blanket thrown over her sleeping figure. She had dark hair, long sooty lashes that swept across her cheeks. She was beautiful. And she was Leon's. Leon and *April's*. That was the woman's name. It made Rose feel sick.

The lawyer was talking, outlining the apparent details of the agreement that Leon had previously made with April. He was sitting there, looking stoic, saying very little. Rose had plenty to say, but it wasn't the time. They were still trying to obscure the fact that Leon had no memory, difficult when he was sitting near a former lover that he clearly didn't have any recollection of. Difficult when he was sitting near a child he obviously didn't remember.

But it was all there, right in front of them. The acknowledgment of paternity, the DNA test and the agreement that April would have full custody along with a certain amount of financial support from Leon.

"I know what we agreed," April said, speaking slowly. "But I find that I'm unable to take care of her. More than that, I don't want to. I thought it would be worth it. Especially with all the money you are paying me, but I just can't. I waited for some…maternal instinct to kick in. Something that would overwhelm me and change me. I'm not changed," she said, sounding sad. Flat. "I could hire nannies, you've given me enough money for that but…I wanted better for her. I'm going to give her up for adoption. But I felt like I needed to speak to you first. I'm willing to sign over all of my parental rights to you."

"She will of course continue to collect a stipend," the lawyer added.

"Of course," Rose said, her tone brittle.

"Yes," Leon said, his tone slightly more sincere, "of course."

"If everything is in order then, Mr. Carides, we are happy to relinquish baby Isabella into your custody."

For a moment, Rose wanted to stand up and shout. She wanted to say no. To send the child out somewhere else, anywhere else but into her home. It wasn't fair. They were making a life together, her and Leon. They were trying to make their marriage work. She was the one that was supposed to have his children. Not someone else. His DNA wasn't supposed to combine with another woman's to make something so beautiful. It should be with *hers*. This should be *her* baby.

She wanted to rail against him. To rail against all of this.

And yet when she looked at the sleeping little girl all she could feel was sadness. It wasn't Isabella's fault that her mother couldn't take care of her. It wasn't her fault that her father had been careless. It wasn't her fault that her father had a wife who felt personally wounded by this indiscretion.

All of the adults in the room had made choices. Rose had chosen to marry Leon. Leon had chosen to sleep with April. April had chosen Leon even knowing he was married. Only Isabella had made no choices.

And no matter how angry she felt, she could feel no anger at the baby. Not really.

"Of course I want her," Leon said, his voice breaking.

He didn't ask Rose what she wanted. But then,

she could hardly blame him. This was his child. His flesh and blood. How could she ask him to do anything but take her into his home? And how could he ever leave the decision up to anyone else? He couldn't. She understood that.

She was still angry.

But she said nothing. She said nothing at all while Leon and April signed the paperwork. Paperwork that didn't include Rose, because why would it? She wasn't a parent to this child. She was only Leon's wife. Why would she matter at all?

"Thank you," April said, her tone hushed. "This isn't my proudest moment."

Rose didn't care at all about the other woman's pride. She found herself short on sympathy.

Leon did not seem to suffer a similar affliction. "You're doing what you think is best," he said. "You should be proud of that."

The other woman tilted her head. "You seem different," April said. "Not that we know each other all that well."

"I stopped drinking," he said, his tone grave. "Maybe that's it."

Then April turned her focus to Rose. And

Rose really wished she hadn't. Rose would rather disappear into the ornate wood paneling on the wall. She wanted to hate the other woman. But when she saw the exhaustion in her eyes, a deep sadness that her flippant *I don't want this* tried to disguise, she simply couldn't. "I'm sorry," April said, her words directed at Rose.

"There isn't anything to be sorry for," Rose said, surprised by the fact that she meant them at least a little bit. "Leon has to answer for his own actions—you don't. *You* didn't make vows to me."

"Well, I think he was trying to keep all of this away from you. But I didn't feel right about putting her up for adoption without…"

"I understand. I'm glad that you came to us." She wasn't sure it was true. But it was the right thing to say.

Without another word, April and her lawyer walked out of the office. April didn't look back again, not at Leon, not at Rose, and not at the child that was still safely buckled up in her car seat.

Rose felt like a small pink bomb had been detonated in the middle of them. They had been making things work. Things had been changing. Things had been different. But the simple fact was that no matter whether or not Leon could remember the past, the past existed. It was so tempting to believe that a clean slate was possible. That because his memories were changed, his actions had, as well. But this was incontrovertible evidence to the contrary.

"We don't have any supplies for a baby," Leon said finally, breaking the silence between them.

"That's what you're going to lead with?" Rose asked, hearing in her tone the fragile nature of her mental state.

"What do you want me to say? I have no memory of any of this. Obviously I knew about the child, Rose—I signed those documents. That is my signature. I signed away the rights to my child."

"A child you had with another woman during our marriage."

"Yes," he said, his tone fierce. "Though it is no surprise to you that I was sleeping with other women."

"It does surprise me," she said, her voice rising along with the hysteria in her breast, "that you had a child with someone else. That's quite the secret to keep."

"I find I am more distressed by the fact that I clearly wanted nothing to do with Isabella."

"Well, I imagine you wanted to avoid this scenario."

"What kind of man does that?" Leon asked. "What kind of man pays a woman off to keep a child out of his life?"

"You," Rose said, not caring if she was cruel. Not caring if her words cut. "Apparently you do."

"I'm starting to think I know nothing about myself at all," he said, his voice hollow.

But she didn't feel sorry for him. She refused.

"The feeling is mutual," she said.

Rose turned on her heel and stormed out of the office, doing what she knew was about the cruelest thing she could. She left Leon alone with his thoughts. And with his child.

Leon stared down at the sleeping baby in the car seat, emotions rolling through him like storm clouds, pressure building inside him. Who was he? What sort of man kept his wife ensconced in a manor house in the country, leaving her a virgin for two years while he lived his life as though she didn't exist?

What sort of man brought a baby into the world and wrote an agreement making it completely clear he never wanted to see her?

He gathered from the paperwork that he had never set eyes on his daughter. He gathered he hadn't even known the gender of the child.

Weariness stole through him, and a darkness rolled through him like clouds covering the sky.

What did you do when you found out you were a monster? Because he had to be a monster. There was no other explanation. Real men did not abandon their children like this. They did not pay to make their own flesh and blood go away.

He didn't know if he had ever held a baby. He had certainly never held this one.

Suddenly, he found himself dropping down to his knees, his heart pounding so hard he could scarcely breathe. He looked at the little girl, sleeping there in the car seat. So tiny, so perfectly formed. Abandoned by the only parent she knew, brought to stay forever with the man who had signed her away as though she was an unwanted object he didn't want cluttering up his home.

"I am sorry," he said, his voice raw, strange. "I am sorry for the man I was. But I will not abandon you. Not now. I will fix this. I will be the father you deserve. I will be the man that both of you deserve."

He didn't know how long he stayed like that, sitting on the floor in front of her, simply staring. But eventually, she began to stir, a plaintive, high-pitched wail on her lips as she came fully awake. Her eyes open, bright blue, not at all what he expected, glaring at him as though he was her enemy. Then the tears started to fall down her angry red face and panic flooded through him.

He picked up the car seat, wincing as pain from his ribs shot through him.

He had to find someone. Anyone. He did not want to pick her up. He was afraid he would break her. He had no memory of how to hold a child. Perhaps he had never known how.

"Rose!" He made his way out of the office and through the halls. "Rose, I need you."

Rose emerged from the library, her face pale, her eyes red.

"What is it?"

"The baby is crying."

"Yes," Rose said, crossing her arms, "she is."

"I do not know what to do."

Rose stayed right where she was, her feet planted firmly on the floor. "I'm not sure what you want me to do about it."

"*Help* me."

She still didn't move. Then finally, as Isabella's cries continued to fill the air, Rose's expression softened. "I'm not going to help you. But I will help her." She crossed the space between them, stopping in front of him. "Put her seat down."

He complied, and then Rose knelt down, beginning to work the harness that kept the baby strapped in.

She undid the seat belt and plucked the baby up from the seat, cradling her tiny body close to her chest. It made something inside Leon's own chest tighten. Made it almost impossible for him to breathe. There was something about all of this that was familiar and foreign at the same time. Something that filled him with a terrible sense of dread that made it feel as though his insides were slowly turning to ice.

He found himself completely rooted to the place he was standing. He couldn't move forward. He couldn't turn away.

"She might be hungry." A tear slipped down Rose's cheek and he despised himself. The two women in his life were here in front of him, weeping, and he could do nothing to stop any of it. He didn't know how. He didn't know how to comfort a baby, and he found himself somewhat terrified by the sight of her. He didn't feel he deserved to try to offer comfort to Rose. Whom he had betrayed.

"Are you all right?" It was the wrong thing to ask. He knew the moment he spoke the words. And it was confirmed by the way her mouth flattened. By the way her eyes cooled.

"I don't know how to take care of a baby. I don't know what to do. This isn't what I want," she said, her voice breaking.

There was no response for that. It didn't exist inside of him. He wondered what he would have said if he was in possession of his memories. He wondered how he would respond to this. How he would respond to her.

"First I will send out some of the staff to buy

supplies," he said. He didn't know what would come next. He realized the way he had begun that sentence implied that he had a list of actions to take. But he could barely wrap his mind around the one.

"That would be good," she said, her tone stiff. "Please just…take her." She took a step forward, thrusting the baby into his arms. He took her, cradling her close. He could do nothing but stare down at her, marveling at the intense shot of fear that gripped him. As though she were a man-eating tiger and not a small girl.

When he looked up, Rose was gone.

And Leon was left alone with his daughter.

CHAPTER SEVEN

ROSE FELT LIKE she was made of pain. She'd spent the entire day curled up in her bed, a lump of misery that could not be moved. She was assuming that Leon had seen to taking care of Isabella's needs. She felt guilty for the assumption. But not quite enough to move from her position in her bed.

It wasn't as though she had any experience with babies. None of her friends had them yet. She was an only child, and she had never done babysitting or anything like that when she was growing up.

She couldn't offer him any help. The house was full of staff. He would figure something out.

She ignored the crushing weight that thought brought. She didn't know how she was supposed to sort through this. She didn't know how she was supposed to forgive this.

But she had shared herself with him. As much

as she had loved him before he'd touched her, she had only fallen deeper since they'd started sleeping together. Since she'd started to hope again.

The door to her bedroom opened and she sat up, clutching her blanket to her chest, in spite of the fact that she was fully clothed. "What do you want, Leon?" she asked, not bothering to moderate her tone as Leon walked into her room, slamming the door behind him.

"Are you going to stay angry with me?"

"Probably," she said.

"There is nothing that I can do about this. There is nothing I can do to turn back time."

"And there's nothing I can do to erase how horrible this feels. I just don't understand. I don't understand how you could do something like this."

He exploded then. Every bit of the rage she imagined had been simmering inside of him since his accident, since his memories had been ripped from him, pouring from him. "I don't know why I would do something like this, either, Rose. I have no memory of any of it. No memory of what reasoning there could have possibly been. Why was I not in your bed? Why did I turn my own child away? I don't know the answer to these questions. Everything is gone. It's a black hole inside me. I can never reach the bottom of it. I can't seem to see anything around me. These are the consequences of my actions, and I understand that. I understand that I'm not innocent because I don't have answers. But it doesn't make this any easier."

She gritted her teeth. Fighting against sympathy. Fighting against any kind of understanding. She held on to her anger like it was a lifeline, and she refused to release her hold. "It doesn't make it easier for me, too. It simply means that I can't even rail against you the way I want to. All it means is that I can't get an answer out of you. No matter how hard I try. Though I doubt you would give me one even if you could remember. That's just how you are. You have been kind to me in the past. But I've been clinging to those memories like they have anything to do with the man you became."

"And who is that?"

"A bored, cynical playboy with a drinking problem. A man who has been given *everything*, and seems to feel *nothing*." She took a deep, shaking breath. "You're a brilliant businessman, but you're a terrible husband. You don't love anyone but yourself, Leon. And it has been like that for a very long time."

He seemed stunned by her outburst. Stunned by her words. Well, that made two of them. But it was true. It was everything that she had buried down deep inside herself. Even deeper than the love she felt for him. When she had talked herself into divorcing him, she hadn't used anger to make the decision.

She had latched on to a kind of world-weary practicality. Forcing herself to face that if after two years they didn't have a real marriage they never would. She hadn't allowed herself to feel anything like the sadness that bloomed deep inside her now. Nothing like the rage that burned hot beneath it.

She was allowing herself to feel it now.

"I was wrong. There is no excuse. The reasons don't matter. I was wrong, and I'm very sorry that I hurt you. I'm sorry that I hurt April. That I had any part in hurting Isabella. I am *sorry*." His words were raw, genuine. But she couldn't find it in herself to care.

"It changes nothing. What good does *sorry* do? Can you give me back the last two years of my life? Can you give me back my heart? I am so tired of you holding my heart. I am a fool. I am the fool who has loved you for the last fifteen years, and you never deserved that."

"I feel you're probably right. That I never have deserved for you to have any feelings for me at all."

"I am right," she said, conviction burning in her words. "You didn't deserve my father's affection, either. The world has been kind to you. I imagine the first time anything tragic ever happened to you was when that other car crossed the centerline in Italy."

He closed the space between them, reaching down to where she was on the bed, wrapping his arm around her waist and pulling her up against him. His dark eyes blazed down into hers. "I deserve all of that," he said, his voice low, soft. "All of that and more. Give me your anger, *agape*. Let it out."

"I hate you," she hissed. "As much as I ever thought I loved you. How dare you do this to me? I did nothing but live my life trying to please people. I was the daughter that my father required. I took care of him after my mother died. I never let him see how I used to cry. I never let him know how badly I missed having a woman in my life. I never let him know how lost I was all through junior high and high school. How lonely I was. Because I didn't want him to worry. I agreed to marry you for his peace of mind, even though I knew you didn't love me." She took a gasping breath. "And I never let you know how much it killed me when you went out with other women. I simply accepted what you handed to me. I licked the crumbs that you threw me off the floor, because I am such a sad, pathetic creature. But I am not *your* creature anymore."

He reached up, sifting his fingers through her hair, holding her head steady, staring down at her. "You cannot possibly hate me more than I hate myself."

"Of course I can," she spat. "I wish you could feel this." She pressed her hand to her chest. "I wish you could feel exactly what you did to me."

Tears burned her eyes, her heart pounding, her entire body trembling. She felt desperate. Desperate to make him understand exactly what she felt inside. Her heart was like shattered glass, the shards working their way into her skin, burning, aching.

She wanted him to feel this. She wanted him to understand. This man who had always seemed so charmed to her. So together. Who seemed to get everything he wanted from life, who seemed to be denied nothing.

Who made her want with every deep, desperate part of herself. Who made her want him even now as she burned incandescent with rage over his actions.

She wrapped her arms around his neck, tilting her face upward as she rose up onto her tiptoes and claimed his mouth with hers. She kissed him with all the anger inside her. She poured all the hatred, all the rage that she had just professed straight into him. Hoping it would burn all the way down. Hoping it would destroy him slowly the way that it was destroying her.

She sobbed helplessly even as she parted her lips, thrusting her tongue deep into his mouth. She hated herself. Almost as much as she hated him. For wanting him even now. For needing to be comforted by him even though he was the one who had caused her all of this pain.

But if it was so easy to turn it off, she would have done it a long time ago. If she could simply decide that she didn't want him, decide that she didn't love him, things would be so much easier.

If she could transfer it all to him, exorcise it from her body, everything would be simpler. She would be free. *Finally.* Instead of feeling like there were chains wrapping around her wrists, around her neck, pulling ever tighter. Binding her to a man who could never give her what she needed. To a love that could never give back to her.

She moved her hands, curled her fingers into the fabric of his shirt, holding tightly to him as she continued to kiss him. He pulled her forward, taking a step back, bringing them up against the wall. Then he flipped their positions, her shoulder blades pressing into the wood paneling.

She slid her hands down to his chest, felt his raging heartbeat beneath her fingertips. She couldn't stand these clothes between them. Couldn't stand secrets between them. Couldn't stand lies, even lies that were lost in the dark spaces in his mind.

She couldn't erase those other things. But the clothes, she could do something about.

She tore his shirt from his body, followed by his jeans, and all the while, he made quick work of what she was wearing. Soon they were both naked, pressed skin to skin, as though they were trying desperately to connect. Trying desperately to get beneath everything between them so they could find some way back to each other.

His desperation matched her own. His pain did, too.

Whatever Leon might have felt about any of this at another time, it hurt him now. That didn't absolve him. Not even close. But it satisfied her. Deep down in the meanest part of her, the part of her that wanted him to hurt, too.

She pulled her mouth away from his, angling her head and scraping her teeth along the side of his neck. He growled, grabbing hold of her chin and straightening her head, leaning in and kissing her before nipping her lower lip.

She returned the favor. Sinking her teeth into his skin before soothing him with her tongue.

He moved his hands down her body then, cupping her bottom, pressed her tightly up against his hardened length. She arched into him, seeking oblivion. Seeking satisfaction.

He shifted, moving his hand down, grabbing hold of her thigh and lifting it up over his hip before testing her readiness. Then he thrust up deep inside her, both of them groaning as he filled her.

It wasn't a gentle coming together. It was fiery. Intense. It was rage, it was need. It was a kind of broken hopelessness that wound its way through the air around them, impressed itself on their skin.

When all was said and done they had something to contend with that neither of them knew how to handle. Once the desire between them was extinguished they would have to find a way to move on from this moment. Find a way to handle the child that was now in their life, in the center of their marriage.

Find a way to either repair this betrayal or go their separate ways.

But right now, there was this. Right now, they had each other. And she clung to him. Held tightly to his shoulders as he pushed her to the heights. As he shattered her completely beneath his touch.

She arched against him, crying out as she found her release, and he let out a hoarse growl as he found his own, spilling himself deep inside her.

And when it was over, when her heart rate returned to normal, she released her hold on him, sliding down the wall and sinking to the floor, allowing misery to overtake her completely.

Leon found himself dropping to his knees next to Rose. He wrapped his arms around her, holding her against him as she wept. She cried because of him. Because of the pain that he had heaped upon her. He held her, even though he had no right. Even though she would be better off with a stranger.

It seemed inappropriate to try and heal a wound that he had caused. Although perhaps there was no one else who could do it. Perhaps it was right really. To pour himself into atoning for his sins.

"I'm sorry," he said, the words feeling frustratingly hollow.

He wished he knew everything he was sorry for. He wished he could give them more weight by being aware of each and every transgression he'd committed against her. He didn't need to know what they were to know that he was sorry, but he wanted to list them. Wanted to feel the full weight of them. And he couldn't. Just another in the long list of growing frustrations.

He wanted to answer for his sins. He couldn't even name them.

He wanted to understand why he had betrayed the woman in his arms. Why he had abandoned the little girl sleeping in the crib in the room down the hall. He wanted answers, and his own mind refused to give them.

He was the only one who knew these things. He couldn't tell himself.

"I'm sorry," he said again, because he had no other words.

"This isn't what I wanted," she said, miserable, broken. "It wasn't my dream to raise a child you had with another woman." She drew in a shuddering breath. "I wanted to have your baby. I wanted you to love me."

"Rose…"

"I sound like a child throwing a tantrum," she said, her voice hollow. She drew her arm across her face, wiping in her tears. "It doesn't matter what I wanted. All that matters is what we have. You have a baby."

"I want her," he said. He did. In spite of the ice block that seemed to grow larger inside his chest every time he looked at her. The fear. The uneasiness.

He had a feeling that even if he was in possession of all of his memories, coming into the care of a tiny baby would frighten him. But with nothing, with no background, with no reference for things like this, he was chilled to his bones.

"I know," she said, her throat tight. "And I couldn't ask you to do anything different. She's your daughter."

"But you don't want her."

"No. That isn't it. I…I've known about you sleeping with other women, Leon. It has always been in tabloids. On gossip websites. It's the world's worst-kept secret. Everyone knows that you aren't faithful to me. Everyone knows that you married a little homebody who can't keep up with you. Who isn't as beautiful as the other women you see." She swallowed hard. "But this... Looking at the evidence of the fact that you were with other women... Knowing that someone else got something I wanted so desperately... It's different. It isn't something I can just brush off."

"I understand that."

"But it isn't Isabella's fault. She hasn't done anything wrong. She's so tiny and helpless, and her mother abandoned her...I can't face the idea of abandoning her. I can't."

"I care about you. You are...the only memory I have, Rose. The one who has been there since I opened my eyes and came back to the world a man with no memory. And I am very sorry for my behavior. But one thing I know...beyond anything... If you feel like you will be angry with Isabella, in any way, if any of your feelings about what I have done might spill onto her... then it would be best if we worked out a different arrangement."

It made his chest feel like it was cracking to

say it. But his daughter would always have questions about what had happened to her mother. And if Isabella had to live in a house where her presence was resented he would never be able to forgive himself. He doubted he would forgive himself for any of this anyway. But for his sins, he had to do something to make it up to Isabella.

He waited. He waited to see if Rose would be angry. She would have every right to be. But it didn't change the truth and what he said. She had every right to be angry. She had every right to punish him. She had every right to leave. But he had to protect Isabella.

"You mean I shouldn't be involved with her if I can't treat her like my own child."

He shook his head. "I can't ask for a promise quite like that. I only mean if you find it impossible not to resent her. If you cannot be in the same room with her. Those things…I deserve them. But she doesn't."

"I know." She blinked. "I feel like I'm being scolded. And you're the one who deserves to be scolded."

"I'm not trying to scold you. It's just… This kind of beginning… If I don't make up for what

I did to her then what future does she have? I signed my rights away. And now I've taken them back, but only because her mother has abandoned her. I never want her to feel like she was a child unwanted by so many. I don't want her to be wounded beyond repair because the adults in her life were too selfish, too broken, to see beyond themselves."

Rose nodded. "I understand. She's just a baby. I'm not angry at her. It was hard for me to look at her. It was hard for me to hold her." Another tear slid down her cheek. "Because I wish she were mine." She pulled away from him, leaning back against the wall, drawing her knees up to her chest. "I wish that things had been different. If they had been, then she very well could have been mine."

"I can't fix the past. I can't even guarantee the future. I can only try and fix what we have now. She can be ours. And I don't say that lightly. I don't say it expecting that you can drop every last piece of baggage you're carrying because of this. I don't say it as though it's a magical fix. But she is here. And so are we. I still…I want to make this work with you."

"Sometimes I feel like you're just going to keep asking impossible things of me," she said, sounding weak, sounding reduced.

"Someday I hope you're able to ask something impossible of me, Rose." He leaned in, cupping her cheek. "And I pray that I am able to rise to the task."

"I want to try." Rose nodded. "For both of us. For all of us. I want to try. Where is she?"

CHAPTER EIGHT

OVER THE NEXT few weeks things seemed to progress slowly with Rose and Isabella. They employed a nanny—a married, grandmotherly sort, at Rose's request—who helped care for Isabella during the day. Though Leon tried to assume as much responsibility as he could. It was just that given the state of things, he wasn't sure he entirely trusted himself. What if he forgot some essential bit of information regarding the care and keeping of babies that everyone else knew? Or, more likely, what if he had never possessed it, but didn't know enough about himself to ask the appropriate questions?

Employing someone to assist had seemed the best option. He could hardly ask Rose to interrupt her life to care not only for him, but for his child.

Still, Rose was beginning to take some charge

of Isabella on her own. When Isabella cried, Rose was often the first to move to comfort her.

Seeing them together made his chest feel like it was being torn in two. Earlier today Rose had been standing by the window, Isabella held tightly to her chest as she stared out at the garden below.

It had been like looking at something much clearer than a memory—especially since he had none that extended beyond the past few weeks. But it hadn't been wholly reality, either. It was a window into a life he didn't truly possess. Something the two of them didn't really have.

In that moment it was easy to believe this was his wife and child, and they had nothing but love between them.

Rather than the dark, tangled mass of lies and betrayal that wound itself around them like a vine covered in thorns. Thorns that wrapped themselves tightly around his gut, making it hurt every time he breathed.

He rubbed his hand over his face and eyed the bar on the other side of his bedroom. It was stocked with alcohol, evidence of the man he'd been before, he imagined. A man who had a drink as he brushed his teeth in the morning and at night.

A man who had sought oblivion with tenacity.

He laughed bitterly, the sound echoing in the dimly lit room. He had his oblivion now. And with it, he found no peace.

Improvement only described the relationship between Rose and Isabella. *Improvement* did not apply to his relationship with Rose. She would not touch him. She would barely talk to him.

He had imagined—erroneously, as it turned out—that after he had held her in his arms while she wept in her bedroom that she might continue to seek out an intimate relationship with him. That was not the case. She scarcely made eye contact with him unless she absolutely had to. She very solicitously inquired about his well-being, never asking about his memories, as she assumed—rightly—that if there were any change he would let her know.

But she didn't look at him the way she had. Those blue eyes, that only real, organic memory in his mind, had changed. They were icy. Angry. Or, on the very worst of days, completely blank. This woman had loved him. And he had destroyed that love.

There were no fresh starts. It was easy to buy into the idea that they'd had one here. That just because he didn't remember what he had done those things didn't exist. But his consequences had now reached their home. Consequences that didn't care whether or not he remembered committing the sin.

That fresh start had always been a lie. He was not a new man, reborn from the fiery wreckage of his accident. He was the same old man. A man who had betrayed his wife, a man who—according to Rose—loved no one but himself. A man who had abandoned his child. He was that man. With Isabella here it was impossible for him to absolve himself in the way he had been attempting to before her arrival.

There was no absolution. He just had to find a way to move ahead. To move ahead desiring the new things that he desired. Carrying the sin on his shoulders, a weight he would try to bear as best he could. A weight he would try not to put on to Rose.

He wanted to walk on, caring for Rose in the

deep, real way he had come to. To try to make her care for him again.

He had a feeling he would have to work hard to earn her affection. As it had taken such a massive betrayal to destroy it in the first place.

It was late now. He would have to worry about these things another day.

He crossed the room and got into his empty bed, feeling a deep ache and loss over the fact that Rose wasn't in here. Not because he would go to bed without an orgasm—though he was not thrilled about that prospect—but because of the reasons she wasn't here. Because of the distance between them that it represented.

But even with that regret looming over him it didn't take long for him to drift off.

He woke with a start. The baby monitor he had plugged into the wall was nearly vibrating with the sounds of Isabella's rage. She was crying in the middle of the night, which she had never done before. Something was wrong. Both he and Rose had baby monitors in their rooms, he knew that. They had decided that given the size of the house it was the wisest thing to do.

But he was going to have to be the one to go and handle his daughter.

He could hardly expect Rose to get out of bed at this hour to deal with a baby that she scarcely wanted.

He made his way out of the bedroom, but each and every step he took down the hall he found his feet grew heavier. A strange, terrified sensation grabbed hold of his chest, freezing his heart, freezing his lungs. He didn't know what was happening to him. His face was numb, his fingertips cold. His mouth tasted something like panic, which was strange, since he wasn't entirely certain panic had a flavor.

The baby wasn't crying anymore. He couldn't hear her. He could hear nothing but the sound of his own heart beating in his ears.

He suddenly felt like he was walking down two different hallways. One in a smaller house. An apartment. And the one he was actually standing in. This was a new feeling. A strange one. The feeling of existing in two places at once, in separate moments of time.

And he realized suddenly, that this was a memory.

The second memory. Second only to Rose's eyes.

It was a foreign sensation. And it was still entirely nebulous. He couldn't grab hold of it, couldn't force it to play out. It simply existed, hovering in the background of his mind, wrenching his consciousness in two.

He tried to catch his breath, tried to move ahead. It took a concerted effort. Perhaps this was what happened to someone with amnesia when their memory started to come to the surface. Perhaps it was always terrifying and foreign. Always immobilizing. If so, then the process of recovering his memories was going to be the death of him. Because this nearly stopped his breath.

He continued to walk, battling against the icy grip of foreboding that had wrapped its fingers around his very soul. He had no idea what he was afraid of. Only that this was fear, in its purest, deepest sense.

The image of the past imposed itself over the present again. Just as he walked into her room, he saw Isabella's crib, and he saw another crib, as well. Smaller, not so ornate. There was no puffy swath of pink fabric hanging down over a solid wood frame. This one was simple. A frail, fragile-looking frame in a much smaller room.

He took another step forward, and found himself frozen again. Isabella wasn't making any sound. And he was afraid to look into her crib.

Suddenly he felt as though he was being strangled. He couldn't breathe. His throat was too tight, his chest a solid block of ice. He was at the mercy of whatever this was—there was no working his way through it. There was no mind over matter. He didn't even know the demon he was fighting, so there was no way to destroy it.

He was sweating, shaking, completely unable to move.

And that was how Rose found him, standing in front of Isabella's crib like a statue, unable to take another step. Terrified of catching a glimpse of his child.

That was what was so scary. He didn't want to see her lying there in the crib. He didn't know why. He only knew that he couldn't face the sight of it.

"Leon?" Her soft voice came from behind him, and he couldn't even turn to get a look at her. "Is everything all right with Isabella?"

"She isn't crying," he said, forcing the words through lips of stone.

"Did she need anything?"

"I don't know."

He heard her footsteps behind him, and then she began to sweep past him and he grabbed hold of her arm, pulling her back. "No," he said, the word bursting from him in a panic.

"What?" she asked, her blue eyes wide, terrified.

"You can't… You can't go to her."

"What's wrong with you?"

"I'm having a memory. It hurts and I can't… I can't move."

She examined him for a long moment, the expression on her face shaded. "I can." She pulled herself free of his hold and moved forward to the crib, reaching down and plucking Isabella up from inside of it.

Terror rolled over him in a great black wave, and he forgot to breathe, bright spots appearing in front of his eyes.

Then Isabella wiggled in Rose's hold and suddenly he could breathe again.

He took a step forward, and the crib mattress

came into full view. It was empty, because Rose was holding Isabella. But yet again, he was seized with the sensation that he was standing in two different places. That he was looking inside a different crib.

He stopped. Closing his eyes he let the images wash over him, along with a dark wave of grief that poured over him and saturated him down deep. It was so real, so very present, so overpowering he felt as though he would never smile again.

And then, it wasn't the same. He wasn't seeing images superimposed over reality. He was just remembering.

Michael didn't wake up for his feeding like he normally did. The silence was what had woken Leon out of his sleep. Amanda wasn't awake. It was all right—Leon didn't mind going and checking on his son.

He walked down the hall quickly, making his way to the nursery. And from there, the vision in his head seemed to move in slow motion. He could remember very clearly being gripped by a sense of dread the moment his son came into view.

And then he reached down to touch his small chest, finding him completely unresponsive.

There was more to that memory. So much panic. So much pain and desperation. He tried to close it all out. Tried to prevent it from playing through to its conclusion. There was no point. Nothing would change the outcome.

And nothing would fill the deep dark hole that was left behind in his soul. The pit that he dumped all of his excess into.

He waited, bracing himself. Wondering if other memories would pour forth in a deluge, overtaking him completely.

As intense as it was to remember anything at all, he would have welcomed more memories. Would have begged for more if the option were available to him. Anything other than being left here with this, and this alone.

He no longer had only empty blackness in him. No, the blackness had been filled. It had been given substance. It had been given form.

Grief. Loss. Death.

Emptiness—he could see now—was a blessing in contrast.

He didn't question whether or not this memory

was real. Didn't question if it belonged to him or to someone else.

It was real, and it was part of him. He knew it down to his marrow. It was such a strange thing to have this memory, with a great gulf between it and the present.

To have the image of that child back in his past so clear in his mind with this child right in front of him.

Suddenly, his legs began to give way and he found himself sinking down to the floor.

"Leon?" Rose's voice was filled with concern.

She placed Isabella back in her crib and turned to him, dropping down to her knees in front of him, placing her hands on his cheek. "Leon," she said, her tone hard, stern, as though she was trying to scold him back to the present.

His breathing was shallow, his face cold. He despised this. Being so weak in front of her. And that realization nearly made him laugh in spite of the pain, because it was always fascinating to simply know something about himself even when he didn't know why it was true.

There was nothing fascinating about any of this, though. Nothing good about this memory.

He wished it could have stayed buried. Of all the things to return to him, why had this returned?

"Michael," he said. It was all he could say.

"What?"

"I had a son. His name was Michael."

Saying that brought back more memories. Amanda. Finding out she was pregnant. The fear. The joy. They had been young, but there was enough love between them to hold it all together.

Until that light had been extinguished.

"What?" Rose asked again, the word hushed.

"I just remembered. I walked in here and I remembered everything about him."

"What happened to him?"

He looked up at her, his chest so tight he could hardly breathe, the words like acid on his tongue. "He died."

Rose looked at her husband, shock and horror blending together, making it difficult for her to process his words. Difficult for her to do anything but sit there in frozen silence as his words cut into her like broken glass. She could feel every bit of pain in them, all of his trauma, his agony.

"You can't have had another child. That isn't possible," she said.

"Do you not know about him?"

"How would I know?"

"I don't know anything about my life, Rose. I don't know what you know about me. I don't… I don't have any idea who I am. Not really."

She swallowed hard. "I didn't know about this." She kept her voice soft, even.

She was angry with him. She had been angry with him from the moment the revelation about Isabella had come to light. She didn't know what it meant for them. What it meant for their relationship, for their future. But she couldn't withhold comfort now. Not now when he looked like a man in the throes of fresh grief.

"Can I tell you?" he asked, his voice tinged with desperation. "Can I tell you before I forget it?"

"You won't forget."

He reached out, grabbed hold of her arm and held her tight. "Someone else has to know. I lost this. I lost the memory of him. Who else knows about him? If I don't tell you… Who else will know?"

She nodded slowly. "Tell me about him."

"Amanda and I were sixteen when we met. We were far too young to have a child. Far too young to have any idea of what we were getting into. And yet that was where we found ourselves. I had come to the United States a year earlier, by myself. I'd managed to find some sponsorship, to enroll myself in school. That was where I met Amanda. Her parents were not impressed that she started a relationship with a broke Greek boy who barely spoke English and lived in his own apartment. No parental supervision."

"I can imagine," Rose said, her voice muted.

"Their concerns were founded. She got pregnant. But we were young and in love, so I imagined that whatever challenges we might face as a result we could overcome." He cleared his throat. "It was us against everyone. And we fought hard. She had a boy—we named him Michael because I wanted him to have an American name. I wanted him to have his place here in this country that I was beginning to love."

He let out a long, slow breath, and leaned back

against the wall. "It is amazing. I'm remembering all this now. It is so simple, but there are
other things…"

"You still don't remember everything."

He shook his head. "No."

"Tell me the rest of the story," she said.

It had a terrible ending. She already knew that.
But it was his story. A blank space filled in not
only in Leon's own memory, but in hers, as well.
She didn't know about his life before he came to
work at her father's company. Didn't know how
he had come to this country. She didn't know
who he was. All of these little revelations that
were coming to light were more and more proof.
Beginning with Isabella, ending with this.

The man she thought she loved was a construct
of her imagination. A man she had imagined
Leon might be.

But of course, she had been so young when she
had first formed feelings for him. In her mind,
he had sprung from the earth fully grown and
handsome, perfect and kind.

A man created to dash away her tears when
she had been stood up for prom. A man designed
especially to stand at the head of an aisle in a

church, looking beautiful and perfectly pressed in his tuxedo as he took her hand and faced her, making beautiful vows to her that she had taken straight to her heart, because she had allowed herself to believe they had come from his.

Now she was seeing the truth of it. He was a man comprised of struggle, of pain. A man who had lived a life full of happiness, loss and untold grief before she had ever met him.

What a shortsighted fool she had been. What a silly little girl.

"Her family would have nothing to do with her or the baby," he said. "I told her I would take care of her. I told her that I had come here to make my dreams come true, and I would make hers come true, as well. She continued to go to school in the few months after Michael was born. I got a job working in the mailroom at Tanner Investments. I paid close attention to the way everything worked, and I started offering suggestions on various different stocks and patterns I was noticing to anyone who would listen. Your father heard about this and allowed me to shadow a few of his best employees while I continued to see to my duties in the mailroom.

I thought…I thought it was the key to changing our lives. To giving Amanda everything I promised."

"I doubt there are very many people on earth who could have accomplished what you did," she said, her voice husky.

"But my business accomplishments aren't really the point of the story. Interesting though they might be." He let out a heavy breath. "Michael died of SIDS in January. He was almost three months old. I have never felt…I am not a man who accepts life. I left Greece, I left my parents, such as they were. I had every confidence that I could make a way for myself here. I believed with great conviction that if I set out to make a home with Amanda, to make a life with her, that we could. And I promised my son that he would want for nothing. And then I walked into his nursery and he was gone." His words were thick, labored as he fought against emotion. "And there was no fighting that. It was too late. Too late. He was gone before I ever knew he struggled. There was no bargaining, no negotiation to be done. I have never felt so helpless. I have never been so aware of the finality that exists in life. Because I was so young and I simply didn't believe rules applied to me. Here I was beating the odds at work, finding my way in this country, but there was nothing that could be done for my son. I was not too special, too strong, or too clever to be defeated by death." His shoulders sagged. "I couldn't help Amanda through her grief, not when I was so lost in my own. Not when I wanted to disappear into each and every new job opportunity that presented itself. A chance to change something. A chance to control something. Of course it wouldn't bring Michael back."

He cleared his throat. "I came home one day and she was gone. I never looked for her. I didn't want a girlfriend anymore. I didn't want someone to care for me. I didn't want to care for them." He closed his eyes and a single tear rolled down his lean cheek. "What kind of father cannot protect his son? If I accomplish all these things, earn money in unimaginable quantities, improve my station in ways others would see as impossible… What does it mean if I allowed my little boy to die?"

"Leon… You didn't let him die. It was a tragic

thing." Emotion was creeping over her, threatening to choke out her words. This was his grief, and yet she felt as though it was a part of her. "It was something you couldn't have prevented no matter what."

He dragged his hand over his face. "I suppose there should be comfort in that. And yet I do not see any. I see only the futility of being at the mercy of fate."

"I'm not sure it's fate. Life is a series of unpredictable things. Beautiful. Terrible. Some are direct consequences for our actions, and others don't make sense. They aren't payments or punishments. They simply are. But the measure of it is what we do after. Those are the things that you can control."

"And what have you controlled? What have you controlled in your life, Rose?" His words were hard, cynical. He sounded much more like the Leon she had spent the past two years married to than he had over the past few weeks.

"Nothing." She blinked back tears. Tears of frustration, of sorrow. Tears because everything about this situation hurt, and no one was left undamaged. "I went along with everything my father wanted from me because I had the idea that if I did he might be happy. That was how I chose to deal with the loss of my mother. I thought you would be my reward. But I'm realizing something."

"What is that?" he asked, his voice sounding rung out, scraped raw.

"Another person can't be your reward. Because they're yet another thing you can't control." She laughed, but nothing was funny about it. "A person isn't cake. They can't just exist to be a treat for you. They have their own baggage. Their own needs and desires. And it wasn't until just before your accident that I started to fully realize that you weren't just going to magically become that reward I felt I deserved. And it wasn't until this that I... Leon, I didn't know about your son. I'm embarrassed to admit how little I know about you. I expected you to be something for me, *only* for me. And I never realized that whatever you were, as broken and debauched as it was...maybe you needed to be that for yourself. For your own pain. I never...I never once considered that."

It didn't fix the past. It didn't make her trust

him. It didn't really even make her forgive him. But understanding that he had suffered a loss greater than any she could possibly imagine did help cast him in a new light. It helped explain some of his behavior. His drinking.

It didn't remove the deep wound from her heart. There was no magic here. Only grim understanding that didn't do a thing to revive the scorched earth that surrounded them.

"I was afraid when I came in here," he said, not addressing what she had just said. "I was afraid that she would be…"

"She's fine," Rose said, knowing that the assurance was empty.

Because she knew what he would always see. She knew what he would always fear as he approached the crib.

And she knew then with absolute certainty why he had signed away his parental rights to Isabella.

"That's why," she said. "It's why you didn't want her."

"If you had asked me what love was after my accident I would have told you…I don't know. But if you ask me now… Love is pain, Rose. It is a hope that blooms with no thought for what might lie ahead. No cares about what could go wrong. And that makes it all the more painful when it's cut away. Devastating. I didn't want this. I didn't want to do this again."

"She's here now," Rose said. And as hard as it had been for her to accept Isabella, she couldn't imagine sending her away. It was a process. There was no getting around that. For Rose, there had been no magical maternal bond between herself and this little baby. But there was something growing in her chest. Blooming, just as he had described it. The beginnings of love.

And protectiveness. She felt that, too. The desire to prevent Isabella from feeling unwanted. Unwanted by Leon or herself.

"Yes," he said, "she is."

"You can't send her away."

"I never said I would," he responded.

"It's my turn to be fearsome about it," she continued. "Things are changing. You are changing. The more memories fall into place, the more you're going to become who you were. And if you think that your original reasoning can stand in light of that—"

"I don't," he said, pushing himself up from the floor, beginning to pace the length of the room.

"And if you do? If you do then I'm going to fight you. Every step of the way. No more secrets. We can't afford to have any between us. This is our life." She was making a stand, a stand she wasn't entirely certain she wanted to make. A commitment. "I want to be a family."

"I don't know if I can promise that."

"You will promise it. You will, or I'm going to have to fight you. For this house. For her."

"You couldn't win a fight against me. As you've already explained if you do not stay married to me for three more years you don't get the house. And as for Isabella… Biologically she's mine. You don't have a right to her."

She was remembering now. Remembering all the ways he could be so impossible. So arrogant. It had been easy to forget because the Leon of the past few weeks had been held at a disadvantage. But this was the man she had always known. Strong. Driven. Occasionally ruthless.

He had done nothing but reveal vulnerability over the past weeks. And she could tell he was fighting now to reclaim these traits.

"So what, then? What is it you want?"

"You will remain my wife."

"And you think you will continue to live as you did? Only instead of abandoning me alone in the manor you'll leave Isabella here, as well?" She stood, closing the distance between them. "That would be in keeping with your past behavior. Shut away the women that cause you grief, that might get in the way of your good time."

"It is not so simple, and you know it. Especially now that you know about Michael."

"Love scares you. *You*, big bad Leon Carides. It terrifies you, and you run from it."

"Only a fool isn't afraid of a lion, Rose. Even I know well enough to be afraid of things that can be fatal."

She was pushing too far. She knew it, but she couldn't help it. "I know you've suffered loss. I know you've suffered pain. But it doesn't give you the right to put other people through hell while you protect yourself."

"You spend your whole life hiding in this mansion, hiding yourself behind the convenient lies you tell yourself, little girl. Hiding in books. You think you know pain because you lost your parents. I buried my *child*. Do not lecture me on pain. Do not lecture me from your safe little nest. You know nothing. Nothing at all."

He turned on his heel and walked out of the nursery, leaving Rose there alone with Isabella.

She debated going after him, but decided against it. She turned and walked to the crib, leaning over the side, letting her knuckles drift over the soft skin of the baby's cheek.

She knew more about Leon now than she had before walking into the nursery. She had a piece of who he was. An explanation for why he was. And yet she felt no closer to him than she had before. If anything, she felt like there was a greater distance between them.

She was beginning to believe that they would never be able to bridge this divide.

The more reality crept in, the more it filled this space between them, the more impossible it seemed they could ever find their way back to each other.

He was not her reward. She thought of everything they had. A broken marriage, loss, pain. She couldn't see the reward in any of it.

She looked down at Isabella again. Maybe

there were no rewards at all. Maybe there was simply life. And what you chose to do with it.

"I don't know that my father ever knew what to do with me," she whispered into the silence of the room. "But I loved him anyway. He loved me, too. He didn't know how to show it, but he did. You see, much like your father he lost someone he loved very much. My mother. I think it becomes difficult after that to show love."

She only realized just now, talking to an infant who didn't understand a word she was saying, that it was the truth. Her father was more comfortable with work, with Leon, because it was simpler than love. Taking a protégé on, helping him succeed...it cost less than loving.

Love was so terribly expensive. And she was only fully grasping that now.

"I loved your father," she continued, a hot tear slipping sown her cheek. "But he's never loved me. That hurts. It makes me want to curl into a ball and never love anything ever again. But I think you're going to need someone to love you. I will. I'll love you like no one has ever hurt me. We didn't choose this. And you certainly deserve better than me. But it's time for me to start making some choices. It's time for me to stop waiting. I choose you, Izzy."

She swallowed hard past a lump that was rising in her throat. "I don't know what your father will do. I can't…I can't make him into the man I want him to be. I can only be the woman I want to be. I can only try to be the mother you deserve. I don't know how to be a mother. I barely remember my own. But I know what I missed having. I can give you those things. He's right about one thing—I do hide. Well, I'm not going to hide anymore."

CHAPTER NINE

THE MEMORIES OF his son had begun to fade back into the past. Shifting from a fresh, sharp grief back into a tender bruise. When they had first hit him they had been as fresh as if it had occurred yesterday, rather than sixteen years earlier.

It had taken him a couple of days to stop reliving it. To stop being hit with fresh realizations.

His son would be a man now, had he lived. Or, at least, on his way to it. He wondered if he had dealt with these realizations on and off in the ensuing years, or if the drinking, the women, were all a part of making sure he *didn't* have these realizations.

He had found that his ability to care for Isabella had suffered. He had avoided her. A behavior he was in no way proud of. But there was no pride in any of this. There was no reason. It was just pain. Pure, unmitigated.

Ever present.

Because, though it didn't hurt to breathe today, the reality still existed in the background. It was part of who he was, this loss. A wound that time might ultimately heal, but one that had most definitely left a scar.

He walked into the study where Rose spent most of her time, where he knew she was cataloging her father's books, and other pieces of his extensive collection. He was surprised to see that there was a little pink bassinet placed next to her chair. She was idly jiggling it as she hummed and took notes, something about the multitasking particularly maternal. Causing a shock wave of emotion to rock him.

"I owe you an apology," he said, the words even shocking him. He hadn't realized that was what he was going to say before he said it.

"Please don't tell me you have more surprises. A bunch of mail-order brides who have just arrived ordered prior to your memory loss? A stable of horses? Gambling debts." She snapped a finger as though a brilliant idea had just occurred to her. "A passel of racing ferrets."

"No," he said, moving deeper into the room, taking his seat on the settee near her chair, keeping a distance between himself and Isabella's bassinet. "Remember when I lectured you on how you needed to treat Isabella?"

"Yes, I believe I do. As I was naked and in the middle of an emotional meltdown. Those moments tend to stand out in your mind."

"It was easy for me to say that to you. That you would have to treat Isabella as your own or remove yourself from the situation."

She arched a pale brow. "Well, I'm delighted that it was easy for you to say. It was not easy for me to hear."

"I imagine not."

"Regardless, it was the right thing for you to say. And I knew it, even then. She's innocent. She has nothing to do with the poor decisions the adults in her life have made. She doesn't deserve to carry anyone's resentment. I might have a right to my anger, but I have no right to direct it at her."

"That is incredibly mature and clear-sighted of you. But I had no right to say it to you. I didn't understand how heavy baggage could be, Rose. Emotionally, I might as well have been a child. Not now. I understand how difficult overcoming anything can be. I'm not sure I have overcome anything of importance."

"Except for the vagaries of the immigration system, poverty and a lack of education?"

"Full points to me for that. However, emotionally speaking…I was in no position to lecture you."

"Is this an honest to goodness apology?" she asked, her blue eyes wide.

"Yes."

"I feel like you owe me one for the other day, too."

"Don't get overly hopeful."

Isabella began to fuss and Rose swiftly put down her notebook, bending down to pick the baby up out of the bassinet, holding her close to her chest. "I feel like Isabella is hopeful she will be getting fed soon."

"Do we…call the nanny for that?"

"No. Elizabetta is out for the day. You're acting like Isabella hasn't been here for the past few weeks. The only thing that has changed is you. You were feeding her. You were taking care of her. Before you remembered."

"The memory is what prompted my apology.

It's easy to see things as simple and uncompli-
cated when you haven't experienced anything."

"I have a news flash for you. Isabella doesn't
care about your pain. She's an infant. She cares
about herself. More to the point, about being
held, being fed and sleeping. She doesn't care
if you're struggling." Rose made no move to get
up. "Her bottle is on my desk in the warmer. Get
it for me."

This was a new Rose than he had previously
experienced. She was being imperious; she was
not being careful with him, or tiptoeing around
his mental state. He found he rather liked it. A
few nights ago in the nursery had been like a
trial by fire. It had been painful, excruciatingly
so, but it had also brought out a fire in him that
had been missing.

Arguing with Rose had felt… Not normal. It
occurred to him then that they never argued.
They hadn't, before his accident. He was sure
about that. That was easy because they barely
spoke. Still, he felt more alive when he was butt-
ing up against her. Perhaps it recalled the way
that he was in his job.

Whatever the reason, it felt like a return to being a man and not just an invalid.

Of course, he felt a lot like a man when Rose kissed him. When she touched him. But she seemed interested in doing none of those things now. So if necessary he would accept fighting as a substitute.

"The longer you stand there the louder she'll scream," Rose said.

He moved toward the bottle warmer, plucked the bottle out of it and handed it to Rose. He was careful to maintain his distance from Isabella.

Rose put the bottle in the whimpering baby's mouth; Isabella made a few grateful sounds as she latched on. Then Rose stood, leaning toward him, "I think you should take her."

He took a step back, his stomach tightening. "I don't think I should."

"You can hold me at a distance all you want, Leon, but you can't do it to your daughter. You dropped your defenses when you remembered your past. You came in and apologized to me, and that was nice of you, but I don't think it was the right thing to do. If you're not going to fight for her, then I'm going to do it. I made a promise. Not for you, not for your sake, but for hers. I promised her that I was going to love her like she was my own child, that I was going to fight for her, and I am. Even if I have to fight you."

He simply stood, staring at her.

"She's a baby. Not a bomb," she insisted.

He had to disagree with that. He knew better than just about anybody that grief was a unique kind of bomb. One that detonated deep inside of you and left wounds that no one else could see. Left shrapnel embedded deep in your soul that you couldn't simply remove.

Children. Your own children had the very greatest ability to damage you simply because of the immediate and intense love they commanded. The protectiveness. That was almost worse than anything else. The need to protect. The gut-rending terror when you failed.

"She is so soft," he found himself saying. "So very vulnerable. I find it…terrifying. I wish I could remember more of myself. I wish I could remember more of my years. As it is, the strongest things are the loss of my son, and the presence of my daughter."

"That must be difficult. You're right. I don't

understand that. I don't understand what it's like to lose a child. It must be…I don't pretend to understand what you're feeling. I won't. But what I do know is that Isabella is here. She needs you now. If you fail her it's because you choose to."

He tasted the strange metallic tang on his tongue, similar to the all-encompassing panic he had felt in Isabella's nursery a couple of nights ago.

"She's here," Rose continued. "She's here, and you've had this accident that might have killed you. This accident that's giving you a chance to change. What's the point of it if you don't take it?"

He reached out slowly then, taking his daughter into his arms, relishing the feel of her soft, warm body against his. She was very alive. Perhaps not something that most people would think about their children. But something he would never take for granted.

"You are right," he said slowly, never taking his eyes off Isabella. He could see himself in her face. In her dark, sharp eyes and her sullen mouth. It was a miracle. To see yourself in a child. Which he was not entirely certain he had appreciated the first time around. But he had been young, and he had not been touched by loss. A baby had been an accident that they were working to contend with. *This* baby was not planned, either. But this baby was a miracle. A miracle he had never thought he'd get a chance to experience again. "I gave this away. I was going to give this up."

"You were afraid," she said simply.

"Do not defend me. I don't deserve it. I was taking the easy way. Perhaps I was afraid because of my experience with Michael, but I'm certain that not wanting to disrupt our marriage came into play. Not for your feelings. For my own comfort. For the protection of my ownership of the company."

She looked away. "You're so certain of that?"

"Like I am about so many things regarding myself. I am certain about this, too. Regrettably so."

"Change it then."

"A fresh start would've been much easier. But that isn't what we have, is it?"

"No. It isn't. But we do have a second chance.

You got another chance to live. You have another chance with Isabella."

As she said that, he realized he wanted those things. And along with it, a second chance with her. Though he wasn't sure he had the right to ask for it.

And he noticed she hadn't listed it.

He had been so determined to try to fix things between them when he couldn't remember what it was he'd done. But once his sins had come to full, horrifying light, he had given her space.

He was through with that. He was through with allowing her to sit back and take her time as she decided what to do with him. He had decided.

He would be the father that Isabella needed. He would withhold nothing from his daughter even with what he remembered.

And he would be a faithful husband to Rose.

Those blue eyes that had once looked at him with so much affection were cloudy now. They were guarded. He would not rest until she looked at him the way she once had.

He was not a man who failed at what he set his mind to.

* * *

By dinnertime Isabella was safely in her nursery, but Rose was nowhere to be found. She had spent the past couple of days avoiding him, but he had always imagined that had he looked for her, she would be easy to find. That was not proving to be the case.

It was eternally frustrating. If he could remember even one thing about her, about the past, then perhaps he might have better luck figuring out where she slipped off to at the estate.

He closed his eyes, picturing the grounds. He had walked all over them in the weeks since his accident. He had nothing else to do.

There were great lawns, a maze comprised of hedges and a few little alcoves with benches and flowers.

Roses.

There was a rose garden that she went to. It was the garden that her mother had planted when Rose was a little girl. That was where she went.

He walked straight out of the house and down a winding, narrow path, closed in with foliage on either side. It was…exhilarating to have figured this out. To know something about his wife.

To realize that somewhere inside of him he did hold knowledge about her. Thoughts about her. Feelings.

As frustrating as it was not to be able to connect more dots, knowing this now was a high unlike any he'd experienced in his recent memory.

Possibly in any memory, but with him it was very hard to say.

The little alcove came into view, a running fountain, large mature rosebushes that were in bloom. And seated on a carved stone bench in front of a bush with crimson roses was the namesake of the flower itself.

She looked up when he came into the clearing, a startled expression on her face.

"I thought I might find you here."

Her mouth dropped open. "You did?"

"Yes. I was thinking about you. And where you might be. And I remembered this garden. Your mother planted it for you. After you were born. Roses were her favorite flower, and that's why she named you Rose. And after she got sick she left this for you."

"I didn't know you...I didn't know you knew anything about me."

He drew closer to her, kneeling down slowly on the ground in front of her, the dew from the grass soaking into his pants. He looked up at her, something about the position familiar, something about the moment echoing in his mind.

He could see her blue eyes, full of sadness, tears tracking down her cheeks as he looked up at her from his position. Here in this spot. In this very garden.

He lifted his hand, cupping her cheek, mimicking what he had done back then. He slid his thumb along her cheekbone, his heart pounding hard.

"This is where you always go when you're upset." He didn't move his hand from her face, and she didn't pull away.

She just stared at him, her cheeks turning a darker shade of pink. "How do you know that?"

He never took his eyes from hers. Those eyes. Eyes he had seen just before his accident. The only memory in his mind when he had woken up in the hospital.

"Prom night," he said, the words coming at the same time as the memory. Just as it had been back in the nursery.

"What?"

"Your prom night."

"I didn't know you remembered that," she said. "What I mean is…I didn't even know you remembered that when you…remembered everything else."

"I do. Your date stood you up."

"My date was a joke to begin with. Nobody wanted to go to the prom with me. I was so weird. And bookish… And afraid of everything."

"You don't seem so scared to me. Not anymore."

She turned her face away from his. "I definitely can be," she said, her voice soft. "I have been. Afraid of my own shadow. You were right when you said I was hiding here."

"I was angry when I said that."

"Yes. But just because you were angry doesn't mean you weren't right."

"We all hide," he said. "We just do it in different ways. I should know."

"What else do you remember?" she asked, her tone hopeful.

"We danced."

Those two simple words opened up a torrent of feeling inside of him. They rocked him. Utterly. Completely.

It was as if the clouds had rolled away revealing an inky, clear evening filled with sparkling stars. And he could see it all clearly.

More than that. He could feel it.

He had gone to the rose garden because he knew she would be there. Because he knew that her date hadn't arrived. And she had been there, crumpled on the bench, sobbing as though her heart was broken.

He had always seen Rose as a girl. Sweet, young. But when she lifted her head and he saw her tear-streaked face, saw the deep sadness inside of her, he saw something more.

And when he had lifted her from her seat and pulled her up against his body, leading her into a dance, he had felt something that terrified him. She was a woman. Not a girl anymore. And he could no longer play off the connection that he felt to her.

Rose. So quiet and serious. Every smile felt earned, every laugh hard-won. And he had lived to earn those things.

He had lived to make those blue eyes sparkle.

He had never wanted to make her cry. And he would bet most of his considerable fortune that he had made her cry more tears than almost anyone else on earth.

"I remember," he said. "I remember coming here. And I held your hand, and it was so soft. And I pulled you up against me and held you close. And you were so beautiful. You were too young for me. But that didn't stop me from wanting you."

She gasped, pulling away from him.

"Did that ruin a nice, innocent memory? I have a way of ruining things. I think we've proven that."

"Nothing is ruined for me," she said, her tone hushed. "I wanted you, too."

"Thank God I didn't know. I fear I would have taken unforgivable advantage of that. I'm not a good man, Rose."

"You are. You *are* a good man… It's just that you've been hurt…"

"How do you defend me? Even now, how do you defend me? If anyone has seen absolute proof that nothing in me is good, that everything I am is deceitfully wicked, it's you. I have been an unfaithful husband. I have been…I have not even been a husband. I was a better friend to you back then."

She shook her head. "What do you want me to say, Leon? Do you want me to say that I think you're terrible? That you've hurt me so deeply I don't know if the wound will ever heal? Do you want me to say that I don't know if I can ever trust you?"

"Yes. Yes, because it's what I deserve."

"But I don't know if it's true. And I won't know, unless we try. I won't know until time passes."

"Time. Bloody, stupid time. I don't have any affection for it at all. What has it given me? It has taken more from me, that's for sure." He laughed hollowly. "Most people grow better. If my memories are any indication I have done nothing but get much, much worse. Until I became nothing altogether."

"That isn't true. The memory that you're having now? The memory of my prom night? It's one of my favorites. Out of all of my memories. And that started out as the worst night… Someone who has the power to take a terrible moment and make it amazing... He can't be all bad."

"Yes, well. While you were wallowing in teenage heartbreak I was imagining pushing your dress up your thighs and burying myself inside of you. And I knew you were a virgin, Rose. I didn't particularly care one way or the other."

"Do you think my imagination was pure?" she asked, raising one eyebrow. "You have no idea how badly I wanted to kiss you."

"I wanted to do much more than kiss you," he ground out.

"I wouldn't have said no."

"I would've hated myself forever."

Her father had brought him through the darkest time in his life. Another piece locked into place. Yes, her father had known about Michael. Leon had confided in him one day at the office. That was the beginning of him taking an interest in Leon.

And he had been the most important person in Leon's world. Rose was a close second. He'd met her when she was a child, and she had delighted him immediately. Realizing she was a woman had been a problem. That night after her prom, he had gone and found a woman at a bar and exercised his sexual frustration with her. Random hookups to keep himself from making any move toward his mentor's innocent daughter.

Because the simple fact was, there was nothing he could offer Rose. She would want love. She would want a husband who could care for her as a husband should. She would want children. He wanted none of those things. He had tried for a family as a young man, and had lost too greatly to ever consider it again.

Rose was so new. So completely untainted by the world that he didn't want to touch her with any of his darkness.

And so he had resisted any pull to her. Any attraction to her. He had buried himself in other women. In alcohol. In all of the usual vices that he used to help himself forget unpleasant feelings.

But one day, his mentor had called him into his office. And he had told him that he was ill. That he was dying. That there was nothing that could be done. Rose was so young; she had always been so protected. And he felt he had failed her as a father. That he hadn't been there for her when she needed him. He had expressed deep, terrible regret to Leon. How he had held her at a distance because of the way he had grieved his wife.

And now, he would never have a real chance to make up for it. He wouldn't be here when she needed him. He wouldn't be here to greet any grandchildren.

He was leaving her, and he wanted to know that she would be cared for.

That was when he had asked if Leon would marry Rose.

He closed his eyes. And he was lost in a memory.

Their wedding day.

She walked down the aisle toward him, her lithe figure displayed to perfection by her designer wedding gown. He took her hand, her father formally giving her to Leon's care.

His throat dried, his heart pounding in his chest. He had spent years denying his forbidden attraction to Rose. Years pretending it didn't exist. And now here she was, being given to him as a wife. He could do whatever he wanted with her. He could finally give in to the fanta-

sies. To the desires that he had always tried to keep in check.

And then it was time to kiss her. He pushed back her veil, revealing her face. Those beautiful blue eyes.

He leaned in, pressing his lips to hers, expecting it to be simple. Expecting to maintain control. She was young and inexperienced, and he'd been with more women than he could count.

But the moment their lips touched, he'd burst into flames.

He was lost in it. In her taste. In her touch. Lost in a way he couldn't remember ever being. And something began to swell in his chest. Something began to shift and change.

And when he had pulled away, he realized he was no freer to have Rose now than he had been before the wedding. That look on her face, that look of sheer joy. Of desire, of… Of love. He could never hope to pay back the wealth that she offered in that look. The deep, rich capacity for caring and emotion that he could see in those beautiful eyes was something he knew he would never be able to match.

And afterward, Rose had gone to their honeymoon suite. And he had not joined her.

He had gotten drunk. So drunk that there would be no chance of finding his way to her. So drunk that there would be no chance he would give in and have her in a moment of weakness.

And she had never come to him. She had never said anything.

Had never begged him to come to her bed. So he had let himself believe it was for the best. That he was making the right choice.

It wasn't until her father had died that he had taken another woman into his bed. He had convinced himself that it was for the best. He had found a brunette. One with dark eyes that would remind him nothing of his wife. But when he had taken her, he hadn't been able to look at her. He had used her. In addition to betraying his wife he had used the other woman.

But just as he had done with feelings, just as he had done with all finer emotions, he continued to sear his conscience until it felt nothing. Until picking up another woman was simply a matter of course, and he could no longer feel any guilt over it. Until he could convince himself that it was nothing more than a game. Until he could force the desire he felt for Rose into the background.

"Why didn't you say anything to me?" he asked, when the torrent of memories finally stopped flowing so freely.

"What do you mean?"

"You wanted me. You wanted a real marriage. After I didn't come to you on our wedding night why didn't you say anything to me?"

She laughed, a hollow, bitter sound. "You can honestly ask me that? Remembering my prom night and the way my date stood me up? I waited for you. But you didn't come. And I would've rather died than ask you why. A man should *want* to be with his wife. She shouldn't have to beg him."

He felt as though he was being torn in two. Regret consumed him. Threatened to overwhelm him completely. The degree to which he had wounded her cut him deeply. The realization of all he had done a destructive force inside of him.

He could say nothing. He had apologized and apologized. It felt empty. It didn't feel enough. At every turn there was new evidence of the way he had harmed her. The ways in which he had betrayed her. He had no words. They were empty. They were fruitless. He could remember making her laugh and smile. Saying all the right things to her. But when it came right down to it he had never done the right things.

He reached up, curving his hand around the back of her head, drawing her down for a kiss. He had no words in him. But he could show her. He could show her what was inside of him.

And if it burned them both alive, he would happily be consumed in the flames.

CHAPTER TEN

HE REMEMBERED.

Those were the words that echoed in Rose's mind as she gave herself over to Leon's kiss.

He remembered that night. And he had wanted her, too.

Somehow, in the years in between that dance and this moment here in the garden, things had taken a terrible turn. Or perhaps, the real problem was that wanting wasn't love. At least, not for a man like Leon. And nothing less than love would ever entice a man to abandon a life of hedonism.

In many ways, that hurt worse than total indifference.

She realized then that it had been very easy to imagine that the real issue was that he felt no attraction for her. As painful as that was, she had imagined that one day she could perhaps make him see her as a woman. That all she had to do was change his feelings and he would look away from other women and turn to her forever.

Now she was faced with the simple truth that he had been attracted to her. It just hadn't been strong enough. He had been attracted to her, and he had resisted her.

It made her ache inside. It made her feel hollow.

But at the same time she wanted to lose herself in this kiss. In this moment. What did it matter what had come before? What did it matter what came after? If she could go back in time to when she was eighteen, sitting here crying, desolate over being abandoned by her date, and grab even one scrap of courage to take hold of what she wanted—to take hold of Leon—she would do it.

She had lived so quietly. So timidly.

She had not gone to him on their wedding night and begged for him because she'd been so afraid of rejection. Because she'd been afraid to face the truth outright, and had preferred instead to cling to hope, no matter how small and hazy it might be.

Where was her reward?

She didn't want to live that way anymore. She wanted to mess up her hair, mess up Leon's suit. She wanted to scream. She wanted to take everything that was on offer and please only herself.

She wanted to change him inside. To affect the kind of landslide that he had triggered inside of her years ago. To leave him altered, to leave him completely and utterly changed for having touched her.

She didn't know if there was anyone in the entire world that was true of. If she had done a single thing to change anyone at all. She was pale, kind of hanging in the background and committed to being inoffensive. Doing her best to keep her head down, doing her best not to be tormented by her peers. Doing her best not to unsettle her father in any way, or cause him any grief.

She was afraid that if she was too loud, if she laughed too much, she would make him sadder. That she would only make him miss her mother that much more.

And the one time she had tried to step outside of that, the one time she had accepted a date at school, it had all blown up in her face.

So she had gone back into hiding. But it had done her no earthly good. She had gone back into hiding, putting her head down, hoping that someday she could convince Leon to care for her, too.

But why would anyone care for a pale little crustacean hiding inside a shell? One that didn't even act like it wanted to see the sun.

But she did now. She wanted to have the warmth of it bathe her bare skin. Here and now out in the garden she wanted the sun to touch her skin; she wanted Leon to touch her skin. And who cared about the consequences?

She had nothing to lose. She had given him her heart years ago and had never gotten it back. She had already been broken by him, broken into tiny pieces so many times it was a miracle she hadn't been blown away by the breeze.

She wouldn't be. She resolved that then and there.

She would become more. She would be filled. With her own desires. With him. She would be too substantial to blow away. Too substantial for anyone to ignore.

She kissed him back. And like every kiss that

had come before it, there was nothing simple to it. It tasted of years of longing, of missed opportunity, of grief and pain. But there was hope, too. Hope for more. Hope for absolutely everything, because the alternative was to exist in silence.

She unbuttoned his shirt, pushing it from his shoulders, baring his chiseled body to her gaze. She placed her fingertips at the center of his chest, moving her hand over his heated skin.

"Nothing is ever as good as you think it's going to be," she said, her throat tightening as she skimmed her touch down over his abs. "Fantasy is limitless. It's also painless. You direct everything. You control all of the movements. Your very own composition." She took a deep breath, inhaling his scent. "Reality doesn't have a place in it. It's like walking in the stars. Knowing that you can't fall back down to the earth."

A rough growl rumbled in his chest. "You make it sound beautiful."

"It's been most of my life. Safe and secure, dreams without consequences." She pressed against the firm heat of his skin. "You never sweat. You never get dirty. You never get injured." She leaned in, pressing her lips to his angular jaw. "And you never reach the heavens. Why walk in the stars when you can go so much higher?"

"Because you might fall," he responded.

She nodded. "I might. We both might. I don't care anymore."

She tilted her head, claiming his lips with hers. It was as reckless, as intense as she was. She vibrated with it. Her need, her desire, coursing along her veins. She raised her hands, grabbing hold of his face, holding him to her as she attempted to quench the thirst that only he could satisfy.

She let her hands drift down to his belt buckle, and that was when she found the control wrenched away from her completely. He growled, reached down and gathering fistfuls of her dress, pushing it up over her hips before tugging it up over her head.

That left her in nothing more than a lace bra and wispy panties, outside in the waning light. She never would have imagined she might do something like this. Ever.

But Leon made her crazy. And she didn't really mind.

She was full with her feelings for him. With her need. Desperate for release.

"Fall with me," she said.

"It might hurt."

She leaned in, pressing her lips to his. "Then we'll be bruised together."

"My main concern is breaking you."

"I think we're already both a little broken." She wrapped her arms around his neck, splaying her hands over his back. "Maybe that's why we fit so well."

"Just a couple of jagged pieces." He brushed his thumb over her cheek. "Except I fear I'm the one who broke you."

She fought against the dry, stinging press of tears putting pressure on the backs of her eyes. Denying this would be easy. Absolving him would be. She wanted to. For his conscience, if for no other reason. But he had broken her. Or at least, he had broken her heart. More times than she could count.

"I think I needed to be broken," she said finally. "So that I would finally start fighting."

She nipped his bottom lip, an echo of what she had done the last time they were together.

When they had fought, and they had made love, and she had cried. That day she had been completely broken in her bedroom. Destroyed as she faced the realization that her husband had betrayed her.

Destroyed as she realized she didn't possess the capacity to be eternally patient. That perhaps she couldn't be eternally forgiving. That, perhaps, in light of that she and Leon couldn't make a future together.

But now she felt like it might be different. Now they were out here in the sunlight together. And it really did feel new. Not because the past was a blank slate. Not because they were starting over. But because they were walking forward.

Because the secret things had been dragged out into the light, and while some of them had proved to be monsters, now that she could see them, she could see how to fight them. Now that she had decided she would stand up and fight.

"You're going to fight me?" he asked, grabbing hold of her hair, tugging her head back so that she was forced to meet his gaze.

"I don't think I could win. In terms of brute strength I'm most definitely outmatched." She fought against his hold, not minding the little pinpricks of pain that dotted her scalp as she did. She pressed her lips to his chest, scraping his nipple with her teeth.

He jerked beneath her touch, growling like a feral beast. Appealing to the wild thing in her. "You plan to use other weapons then?"

She looked up at him, and she smiled. She felt powerful. More powerful than she ever had in all her life. She felt his muscles shift beneath her touch and she scraped her fingernails across his abs, scoring his skin lightly.

His expression was that of a man carved from stone, his entire body gone rigid beneath her touch. Suddenly, she was overcome with a desire to taste him. With the need for it.

She leaned in, tracing a line down the center of his abs, tasting salt and skin and Leon. She was starving for him. She didn't know how she would ever get enough.

She had been with him when he didn't have memories of who she was. She had been with him when she was angry. But this was different. This was different in every way.

This time, when she put her hands on his belt

buckle, he didn't pull them away. This time he let her undo his belt, let her pull the zipper on his pants down, exposing himself to her. The breath rushed out of her lungs, desire replacing it.

She leaned in, flicking her tongue over the head of his arousal. He stiffened, grabbing hold of her hair again, pulling her away from him. "Don't," he said, his words hard.

"Why not?"

"I don't deserve that."

"Life isn't about what we deserve. Sometimes it's just about what people want to give. Or don't. You were never my reward, Leon. And I'm not yours. This isn't a reward. But it's what I want. I want to taste you. I want to be filled with you. Let me."

She took him deep into her mouth then, his harsh groan of pleasure washing over her as she slid her tongue down his length.

He clung tightly to her as she continued to pleasure him. As she gratified herself. Because she made him shake. Because he wanted this. Because he wanted her. Because there was a time when he had not wanted her enough to take her, when he had been able to resist.

But that time wasn't now.

She tasted him until his thighs began to tremble, until his whole body was shaking with pleasure. And then, just as he was about to lose control completely, he pulled her away. He stripped her of the rest of her clothes and laid her down in the grass, the sun washing over her skin.

He kissed her deep, hard, kissed her as he thrust deep inside her, joining his body to hers. There was a rock just beneath her shoulder blade, and it dug into her skin. She knew it would leave a mark. But it was perfect in a way. Because this wasn't gentle. It wasn't clean. It would leave a mark deep down in her soul, and she felt like her skin should bear the evidence of it, too.

She wrapped her legs around his lean hips, urging him to go deeper, to go harder.

His each and every thrust sent a shock of pleasure through her, and she refused to remain silent about it. She encouraged him, told him just how much she wanted him. Just how good he was.

She gasped as her climax washed over her,

shuddering out her pleasure as it consumed her completely.

And as she lay there with him, naked, un-ashamed, exposed in the sunlight, she knew she could never go back to the way things had been. She knew she could never go back to being in-visible.

Right here in this place where her love for him had been cemented, she'd found something new. Love for herself. A need to have more than a quiet, nonconfrontational existence.

Even the way she was planning to leave him had been too easy. Because even leaving him possessed no risk. Kept her hidden.

Kept her from revealing just how much she cared for him.

But here and now it was all laid out in the open. And she wasn't ashamed.

He rolled over, cupping her cheek. "It's time for dinner. That is actually why I came to find you," he said, his voice gruff.

"I guess we had dessert first," she said.

He laughed. Genuine. Real. Balm for her soul. "I guess we did." He pulled her close, his hands drifting over her curves, his touch hotter than the sun. "We should probably go in."

"I don't want to," she said. "I want to run away into the mountains. And then we won't have to do anything. It won't matter what you remember, or what the papers say. You can grow a beard and chop wood."

"Would you like me to grow a beard and chop wood? I could. But I don't think we should move to the mountains."

"Why not?" she asked, pretending to sound tragic.

"Because our home is here. Our family is here."

His words tapped into a well of longing that expanded in her chest. Deep. Intense. So very needy it stole her breath. "You're right," she said. "It is."

"I take it you want to…try?"

She knew what he meant. To try for a marriage. To try and be a real family. "Yes," she said. "Yes, Leon. I do."

This vow was deeper than those she'd spoken at their wedding. Because then, she hadn't known all they would face. Hadn't known how he might hurt her. How he would heal her. Then, she hadn't truly known how deeply she could care. She hadn't known how much it might cost.

But it was the cost that made it valuable. It was the cost that made her *yes* matter.

When they walked back into the house, it was the first time it felt like theirs. And it was the first time she truly felt like Leon's wife.

Leon's memory continued to improve over the course of the next few weeks. Filling in gaps that had previously been vacant. And it was a good thing, too. Because it was time for him to get back to work. He could no longer leave his company unattended and expect that it would thrive. He was in the business of investments, and he knew well just how fraught the market could be. Truly, it was a miracle that everything had been left standing in his absence.

He was beginning to do a little bit of work from home, and he hadn't destroyed anything. Now that he was certain he wouldn't break things simply by touching them, he was beginning to feel a similar level of confidence in his dealings with Rose. Though he was slightly less confident on that score. She was so beautiful. Fragile, and easily bruised much like her namesake. He wanted no part in harming her in any way.

At least, no more than he already had.

Those memories, the memories of how he had treated their marriage, were the most difficult to reconcile.

He still couldn't remember April, Isabella's mother. Couldn't specifically remember dealing with her when she had told him about her pregnancy. He could only make assumptions. He was consigning a certain amount of memories to that file. Memories he would simply have to forget ever existed.

He knew enough now to function as Leon Carides. He knew enough to see to his work. To be a father. And to be a husband. He didn't need anything else.

Rose walked into the studio space that they were beginning to share more often than not. He was holding Isabella as he sought to work on his computer. He had missed so much time with her, he liked to make it up when he could.

"I thought I might find the two of you in here."

"I'm never anywhere else," he responded.

She smiled, her expression almost sad. "That's going to change. Soon you'll be going out and going to work. Probably traveling again."

He frowned. "Yes. I was thinking about that. I see no reason why you and Isabella can't travel with me. I know you've been working to archive your father's writing. To compile your family history. But surely once you have a good amount of that digitized you can start to travel away from the manor."

"Yes. I don't see any reason why I can't." The offer made her glow; the response made him warm in his chest.

"Well, that's settled then. Of course, this is assuming that you aren't sick of me."

"Not even a little bit," she said, treating him to a smile that he knew down in his bones he didn't deserve.

"I have also been thinking about the fact that we never did have a party here in the manor. I know it isn't Christmas. But I will be returning to work. I'm going to need to put on a strong face. Of course, most of the world doesn't know about the exact effects my accident had. But I am going to have to put on quite a show to restore confidence in my abilities as an investor. Beyond that…there is the small matter of introducing Isabella as part of our family."

The look of pain on Rose's face stole any warmth that had just lodged itself in his chest a moment ago. "Of course we will," she said, her tone practical.

"It is a necessity. But of course, the world will not believe that you secretly gave birth to a child. I'm going to have to confess my indiscretions."

She nodded slowly. "And I suppose I'll stand behind you like a dutiful wife as you make the claim."

"You do not have to stand behind me. You can stand in the crowd and throw rotten fruit if you like."

She shook her head. "No. I'm not going to do anything that would cast you or our family in a negative light. No, we can't hide the truth. Obviously, Isabella isn't my baby. And, honestly, if we tried to maintain that fiction it would only come crashing down around us later. Nothing is going to stop April from coming forward if she sees the potential opportunity for a payday. She didn't seem like a terrible person, but she did seem like a woman who might find herself in desperate straits eventually. We don't want to open ourselves up to that. The truth is the only way forward."

It had been true for the two of them; of course it would continue to be true for their family.

"I agree. We will release a statement, but quietly. After our party."

"You want to have a party?"

"Yes. With my beautiful wife by my side. A statement. Of my commitment both to you and to the business. A show of how things are changing after the accident."

"I see. And what will you tell the public?" she asked.

"Simple. I will tell them that you nursed me back to health. I will tell them that my brush with death caused me to reevaluate some things. And that I have changed. All of these things are true."

"Yes. Just leaving out the part about the amnesia."

"I feel that amnesia is best left unmentioned."

"That is probably true. First of all, I doubt very

many people would believe it," she said, wrinkling her nose.

"We are rather like a bad soap opera, aren't we?"

She crossed the space, coming to sit down beside him, and pressed kisses on his cheek. "With a little bit less tragedy, I hope," she said.

"One can only hope."

"Then, I suppose we are going to be very busy planning a party," she said.

"Or rather, the staff will be. I would rather keep you busy with me."

Rose smiled. "That can be arranged."

CHAPTER ELEVEN

PUTTING ON FORMAL dresses never did end well for Rose. That was why she was unaccountably twitchy and deeply uncomfortable as she zipped up the crimson gown, smoothing the silky fabric, watching the weight conform to her figure. First there was her prom. Then there was her wedding. And now this.

It made her feel a deep sense of encroaching doom. It made her feel so uneasy she could hardly breathe.

She looked at her reflection. At the wide-eyed woman staring back. She was expertly made up, shadow highlighting the blue of her eyes, her lips a deep crimson.

But she still saw plain, bookish Rose. Who would have to go downstairs and stand next to Leon, who couldn't be called plain or bookish in any circumstances.

She took another breath. It would be fine.

This was different. This was their first party as a married couple. This was a symbol of Leon's commitment to moving forward with her. This was their new beginning. And yes, eventually, they were going to have to deal with the fact that they had to tell the world about him having a child with another woman. But, for tonight, they would just have their party. For tonight, Leon would show off his improved health, and they would stand together, truly a couple for the first time in the eyes of the world.

She took a deep breath, looking down at Isabella, who was in the small bassinet that was currently in the room she shared with Leon. The baby was sleeping, and Elizabetta would be upstairs to ensure that she was taken care of during the party.

Still, it was Rose's first instinct to stay hidden up here with the baby. Mostly because she was used to hiding. Used to staying out of the spotlight. Out of the way.

She was used to watching from upstairs. She was definitely not used to being down in the party.

"Well," she said fiercely to her expression. "Tonight you are."

The bedroom door opened and Leon walked in. Her heart slammed against her breastbone, her mouth going dry. He looked beautiful in his perfectly fitted suit, all traces of the vulnerable, confused man she had spent the past couple of months caring for erased. This was the Leon she had always known. Confident. Suave. Perfectly at ease in any situation he might be dropped into.

"Rose," he said, his dark gaze intense. "You look…I don't have words. There is nothing that will do you justice."

She felt her skin heating all over. "Thank you."

"Shall we?" He extended his arm, and she looped hers through it. Then they continued downstairs together.

The ballroom was already full of guests, men who looked exquisite in their tuxedos, women who were resplendent in their gowns. That earlier insecurity that was vibrating over her body grabbed hold, worked its way beneath her skin.

He had said there were no words for her beauty, and yet there were so many women in here who possessed a much richer, deeper beauty than Rose did.

The kind of women he used to prefer to her.

He had spent nearly two months with her as his only lover. Surely these other creatures, rare hothouse flowers—that were nothing like the common garden variety of bloom that she was— held greater appeal.

Perhaps that was why he had no words. Because she was simply plain.

At some point, she scolded herself, tightening her hold on him, *you have to trust him.*

Yes, at some point she would. But it was difficult. Not because he hadn't proved himself to be loyal over the past couple months. Simply because these months were like something out of a dream. And when it all came down to it, he had not offered her the most important thing. He had promised commitment. He had promised it several times over. But he had never offered feelings. He had never offered love. That concerned her.

Attraction was one thing. It was most certainly real. At least between the two of them. At least… for her.

What would happen when that changed? What would happen if she were to become pregnant with his child? If her body changed? What would happen when she aged? Would his feelings change along with her appearance?

She pushed the thought firmly into the back of her mind. She was not going to focus on anything like that. She wasn't going to doubt him. Not now, not when he had given her nothing to doubt.

A man in a perfectly cut suit, with a beautiful woman on his arm, crossed the space between them. The woman was visibly pregnant, although her bump was neat and small, making her look rather serene and elegant. And she was very much in love with her companion.

"Carides. It is good to see that you're unharmed."

She could see by the relatively blank look on Leon's face that he was not entirely certain of who he was speaking to.

"We haven't met," Rose interjected. "I'm Rose Tanner. I'm Leon's wife."

At that, the man's beautiful companion blinked.

"Nice to meet you," she said. "I'm Charity. Charity Amari. This is my husband, Rocco."

"Charmed," Rocco said, reaching out and taking her hand, pressing his lips to her skin.

She could see something change in Leon's expression. "The last time I saw you was just before my accident," he said.

"Yes," Rocco said. "I'm glad to see you weren't killed. Though I did find myself a little bit irritated with you as you did such a good job of charming my wife."

Rose looked at Charity, then down at the baby bump. Charity laughed. "That is definitely my husband's doing," she said. "Not yours. I was not as charmed as Rocco feared I might be. But since I was feeling rather uncharmed by him at the time, he had cause for concern."

"My own fault," Rocco said. "But all is well now. As it seems to be with the two of you."

"Yes," Leon said, taking a step toward Rose and wrapping his arm around her waist. "One thing my accident showed me was that I was taking my wife for granted. I will not do so anymore."

Rose couldn't help herself. She turned to look at her husband. "Why?"

He frowned. "Why what?"

"Why won't you take me for granted?"

She knew what she wanted to hear. She didn't know why she was pressing for it now. But it was too late to turn back.

"Because, *agape*. You're very important to me."

"Why?" she insisted.

"Oh, dear," Charity said. "I do think you might be in a bit of trouble, Mr. Carides."

"That is nothing new," Leon said, his tone smooth. Clearly, he was no longer uncertain of how he knew the Amaris.

"Well, I suggest you find a way to fix it," Rocco said. "I'm glad that I did."

The two of them turned and walked away, and left Rose alone with Leon.

Jealousy was like a fire-breathing dragon inside of her. "Would you care to explain to me exactly how you know her?"

"Jealousy, Rose? You know perfectly well that I committed sins before my accident. That has been made abundantly clear. But if you suspect every woman we come into contact with—"

"I have every right to suspect her. We've been living in a dream world, Leon. Everything between us has been so easy. Because we've been here alone."

"We have not been alone. If you will recall we had a visit from one of my former mistresses. And it has not been easy. As you will also remember she came to give me my child."

"I have not forgotten."

"You think so little of me that you think you have cause for concern just because other women are parading themselves in front of me?"

"When have you earned anything else?" She despised this small, mean part of her that was lashing out at him now. It was all of the insecurity. Roiling inside of her like a beast.

He shook his head. "I haven't. But at some point, you will have to allow me to try without constant suspicion."

"Just answer my question."

"I met Charity at an event the night of my accident. She was firmly and fully besotted with the man she has now married. She had no interest in me."

"But you tried to see if she might?"

"Mostly to make Rocco angry. I find him insufferable."

"You remember him now."

When Leon had a memory, it tended to come in waves. She wondered which other memories would be visiting them tonight. She should have known there would be new memories. After all, they would be encountering people he had interacted with in the life that extended beyond the one they had created here in the manor. This truly had been a cosseted existence, one she hadn't fully appreciated until now.

Now she was sharing him with the world. This man who had become so essential to her. She had always cared for him, but now that they had become intimate it was different. Now he felt like he was a part of her. And allowing other women to look at him, allowing them to get anywhere near him… It was much more difficult than she had anticipated it might be.

There were women here who would remember what it was like to be with him. Who would remember what he looked like naked. And he would have similar memories of them.

She really hadn't appreciated how hard that might be.

"Do you remember anyone else?"

"Is that a rather snappish way of asking if I have ex-lovers here?"

"Yes," she said, her voice near to a hiss.

"You have certainly changed, Rose. You used to be much more biddable."

"New things you're starting to remember?"

"Yes."

"Who knew this party would be such a treasure trove."

He grabbed hold of her arm, stopping her from walking away, turning her toward him. Then he reached out, gripping her chin between his thumb and forefinger. "What we have has been good. Do not ruin this."

"How can you accuse me of being in any danger of ruining it? I'm not the one who took lovers during our marriage."

"No. That was me. I am the one who took lovers during our marriage. I did not hide it. I am ashamed of it. I am also the one who cannot change the past. And so, *agape*, I would ask that if you wish to be in a marriage with me you allow me to move on from the mistakes that I have made. For if you never allow me to be more than that, then how will I ever transcend it?"

"It's on me now?" she asked, her tone icy.

"If you want to be with me," he responded. "If I can never be anything to you but the man who betrayed you then I don't see how we can move forward."

His words hit her square in the heart. "I'm sorry."

She had been nervous from the moment they had arrived down here at the party. She wasn't acting like herself. And it wasn't fair to him.

"Can you tell me what the problem is?" His voice was tender, his eyes soft. It made her feel terrible.

"We don't need to have this discussion now."

"I fear that we might. Especially as you seem so very upset with me."

"I'm not upset with you. But…I can't forget the fact that you were happy to sleep with every woman in this room except me for the past two years. And yes, that makes me a little bit insecure. And it's much easier to be angry at you than it is to feel that insecurity."

"You are exaggerating. I did not sleep with every woman in this room."

"Oh, really?"

"A third of them. Maybe. And that's being generous."

She laughed, in spite of herself. "All right. So maybe I'm being a little bit overdramatic. It's just… It's hard for me to believe this is real. Everything has changed so much. You've changed so much. And I suppose I'm afraid that you'll wake up and everything will change back."

He tipped his head to the side, his dark eyes glittering with intensity. "I'm not asleep, Rose. I'm not going to wake up from anything."

She nodded slowly. "Okay. I think I understand that. But it isn't as though there is a guideline for dealing with things like this."

"Yes. Sadly, the *So Your Spouse Has Amnesia* handbook has been out of print for quite some time."

"It really is a shame. Women like me could use some guidance."

"Well, I'm all out of guidance. Why don't we dance?"

He took her hand and led her out into the middle of the dance floor. Rose allowed herself to be swept into his arms. For a moment, she felt like she was lost in one of her childhood dreams. The ballroom was ornately decorated, the music swirled around them. Her husband, so strong, so impossibly handsome held her close. And when he turned her, she could see straight through the ballroom doors, up to the top of the stairs where she used to sit, crouched and watching as her parents did the very same thing.

Finally, she was a part of this life that she had dreamed of for so long. She felt like she was standing in a dream. And she knew there was only one thing that would make it even more perfect. The one thing that was causing the trouble tonight.

It was a risk. She knew it was. But she was ready to take it. Here, lost in this beautiful moment that seem to be comprised almost entirely of stars, she felt as though she could never fall down to the ground. And if she did, surely he would catch her.

"Love," she said, her voice soft. "It's the lack of love that's concerning me. I love you. I love you so much, Leon, and I want very much for you to love me, too. That's what I need to be certain. That's what I need to trust. Love."

He went stiff beneath her touch, his black eyes taking on a hollow quality.

The world as she knew it fell away, the stars burning out. And Rose fell down to earth.

CHAPTER TWELVE

LEON WAS LOST in a memory that he had tried very hard to keep at bay. It was the look in Rose's eyes that had done it. That earnest sincerity. It was imagining that that had propelled him forward during his discussion with April a little more than a year ago. He had been imagining what Rose might look like when he told her he had gotten his mistress pregnant. Because it had *absolutely* occurred to him to fob the child off on his wife. After all, he was never home. He wasn't intimate with Rose. But surely she wanted a baby.

That thought had stopped him short. Because there was no way the baby could be in his house and he could keep himself from forming an attachment to it. He knew well enough that babies had a way of crawling beneath your skin. Of overtaking you completely. And of ripping your heart out when loss invaded your beautiful family.

"I'm pregnant, Leon. And I'm not going to get an abortion. So I don't know what you want to do about it. But I can't raise the baby without support—"

"I'll pay you. Whatever you need. But I'm not going to take care of the child. If you need support putting it up for adoption, that's up to you. Otherwise, I'm more than happy to set up funds so that you can make sure that you are both cared for."

There was one thing he knew for certain. He could not undertake raising another child. He had never, ever intended to put himself through that ever again.

He hated himself for being so irresponsible. For putting himself in this position. But he was a man with money. And he could pay to make it go away. There was no reason on earth he would ever have to see the baby. He could pretend it had never happened.

And so he had established the paperwork, come to an agreement on the amount and promised to give April full payment once paternity had been established. He had never seen the child. He had been notified of its birth, and he had asked that she not tell him whether it was a boy or a girl.

He'd wanted to know nothing about it.

But the night of his baby's birth, he had gone and gotten as drunk as he could remember ever getting. There wasn't enough alcohol on earth to drown out the pain. And he had wished more than anything that he might find solace in Rose's arms. Because there was something about her that had always seemed like home. Something about her that had always seemed like she might be the resting place he had wished for his entire life.

And it had been all the more reason to stay away from her. He had found another woman. A woman whose face he couldn't even remember. And that had been so much the better because she hadn't been special. He didn't deserve special.

He snapped back to the moment and Rose was still staring at him, her blue eyes filled with concern. With pain.

"What did you say?" he asked.

"I love you. And I want for you to love me back."

He could see the truth in her blue eyes, and it was all too harsh. Too clear and bright. It was everything he'd always feared.

That honesty. Real, and deep. Reaching out for him. Asking for it in return.

He realized it then, as he stared back at her. She was everything pure and true, and she always had been. While he was a lie. Down to his very core.

He did nothing, not a single thing, with a shred of honesty. He lied to everyone. To his wife, his mistresses, himself.

No wonder he had lost his memories so easily. No wonder they had slipped away into the darkness with such ease. They were nothing.

He was nothing.

His mind was full now, but his hands were empty, and she wanted him to give her something that he…he simply couldn't.

He released his hold on her and began to back away. Then he turned, walking out of the ballroom, straight out into the entryway of the house, and out the front door. A summer shower was pouring down, large drops of water splashing on the paved drive. He looked around, desperate for escape. Desperate for reprieve.

"Leon!"

He turned, and saw Rose standing there in the doorway, her pale petite silhouette backlit by the golden light coming from inside the house. He knew right then she was everything he had ever dreamed of. She was warmth. She was light. She was home. And he could reach out and take none of it.

"No," he said, his voice rough.

"Leon, don't go."

"We cannot do this."

"Like hell we can't." Rose picked up her dress, holding the red silky fabric balled up in her fist as she made her way down the steps, and out into the rain. It fell across the gown, leaving dark splotches on it, as though she were bleeding out right there in front of him.

A wound for his every word.

He had hated himself. Hated himself for a long time, for a great many things, but he'd never hated himself more than he did in this moment.

"I can't," he bit out. "And there is the final

piece of my memories. I can't love you. That's why I never touched you. That's why I was never supposed to. That's why it was better for me to spend the past two years warming the bed of every woman who would have me, rather than ever touching you. Because for all my sins, Rose, I never intended to hurt you."

"But you did hurt me. You always hurt me. From the moment you agreed to marry me and then never touched me you hurt me. So it's too late to pretend that you had any kind of self-sacrificing notion when you married me. You might have felt guilty, but surely you must've known you were going to hurt me."

"I thought…" he ground out, the rain splashing down his shirt, sending trickles of cold water down his skin. He didn't care. "I thought," he continued, "that I might be able to have you. I thought perhaps I could condemn my conscience to hell and have what I pleased. I wanted you, Rose, make no mistake. Were it only down to attraction I would have had you on your back when you were eighteen, as I already told you. But it was more than that. Your father trusted me, and I knew that I could never give you what you would want."

"And you thought you knew what I wanted?"

"Yes. You want this. You want love. You want things that I can never, ever give. You would stand there and tell me that I'm wrong? Even as you prove me right? You cannot do that."

"But things have changed. You have Isabella… You have *me*. Surely…"

"I remembered," he said. "I remembered when we were in there. When April came to me to tell me she was pregnant. If only my reaction were one half so steeped in grief as I imagined. I did not want the responsibility. I couldn't bear it. My life was perfect. I was a carefree bachelor with everything I wanted. Never mind the fact that I actually had a wife. You were a wife that I never had to see, a wife that I never had to speak to. Out of sight, out of mind. I had established for myself a perfect life. And, while I considered taking the child and giving her to you to raise, since I certainly wasn't going to get you pregnant, I decided in the end that perhaps you wouldn't take so kindly to that."

"Leon…"

"It started with grief, Rose. It definitely did. But it twisted me into a cold, selfish man, and by the time I rejected my own child that was the only thing that was driving me. I lost the capacity to love. I felt no sadness signing away the rights to my flesh and blood. Do you think I once mourned the fact that I wasn't in your bed? Do you think I felt even the tiniest sliver of guilt when I took another woman into my arms in spite of the vows that I spoke to you? I didn't. I could pledge faithfulness. I know that I can. I don't want the things that I did. I find that I'm satisfied with you. Love? I don't love anything. I'm never going to love you."

The words poured from him, a toxic kind of black ooze that covered everything it touched. He hated himself. He hated her even more for asking this of him. For making him hurt her. For making him destroy this beautiful thing that they had built between them. But he couldn't love her. He couldn't.

Already, there was Isabella. And he loved her in spite of himself. Perhaps, she would even love him in spite of himself. But…when he looked at Rose, when she demanded love from him, there was nothing but fear. Loving Isabella… Loving Rose… If he did that and he lost them, it would bleed him dry. There was no way he could ever endorse such a thing.

"Leon, I know you love me."

"No," he said, his tone final. "I don't."

"But these past few months…"

"When we began a physical relationship it was when I had no memory. I had no idea who you were. I had no idea who I was. But I know now. I am simply a man too scarred, too damaged to ever care for anyone. I am not the man you wish I was. I'm not even the man I wish I was. I can promise you faithfulness, but I cannot give you love."

"A promise doesn't mean anything without love."

"Then that is your decision," he said. "I cannot make you change your mind."

"So you're telling me I should simply believe you? With nothing else but your word?"

He saw it then. The chance to do the right thing. For the first time in too many damn years. He met her gaze, watched the rain pour down her beautiful face. And he memorized her. Memorized every slope and curve of her face. Memorized that exact color in her eyes, and deeper, the way they looked at him now. With hope. With love.

One last moment before he drove it all into the ground.

"You are right not to trust me, Rose. Very few things matter to me less than the truth. I know who I am now. I'm Leon Carides. I was a boy in Greece who hated his impoverished life and lied his way into the US. Who seduced a girl from a nice family and promised to care for her, and instead devastated her existence. Who married his mentor's daughter with no intention of ever honoring his vows. Who had a child with a lover whose name he barely knew and was so comfortable piling deceit on yet more deceit he thought nothing at all of concealing it from the world. From his *wife*. I don't even know what the truth is. Much less love."

"I want to show you," she said, the light still shining in her eyes.

"But I won't be able to see it," he said.

"I told you once that you asked the impossible of me. And you said—" her voice broke "—you said someday I could ask you for the same. And that you would try. Why won't you try?"

Something broke inside him. Or maybe it was already broken. Maybe now he just remembered that it was. "Because I don't want to."

And with that, he extinguished it. Finally. With that, she turned and left him, standing alone in the rain.

She left him there with all of his memories, all of his pain.

And he simply stood there, and longed for that moment when the only thought in his head had been Rose.

When they had simply been the truth. And there hadn't been a single lie in him.

He had loved her then.

He realized that now. When everything else had fallen away, he had loved Rose. There had been nothing to stop him then. When he was clean, and new. There had been only him, only her, and loving her had been both instant and simple.

But with each new memory that crowded in, each new wound reopened, he'd found love pushed further and further away. Until it was out of his reach.

Until he envied a man lying broken in a hospital bed without a single memory beyond his wife's blue eyes.

Rose couldn't face going back into the party. Instead, she turned, leaving Leon standing there in the rain, and ran. She didn't realize quite where she was running to until she found herself in the rose garden. She knelt down in front of the stone bench, not caring that her dress was getting soaked. Not caring that it was getting dirty. She laid her head across the hard, cool surface and allowed her tears to mix with the drops of water that were falling from the sky.

She felt hollowed out. Hopeless. She felt utterly and completely alone.

She shivered, cold and panic washing over her in equal measures.

This was the thing she feared the most. Being alone. Demanding so much that the person standing before her would decide she wasn't worth it. It was why she had never demanded her father pay attention to her. Why she had never done anything but play the part of meek, solicitous daughter.

Why she had never once commanded Leon treat her more like a wife, rather than like she was invisible. Why it had taken her so long to get to the point of asking for a divorce.

Why she had preferred a divorce, *running*, to asking him to be her husband. To asking for what she wanted. Because she had been afraid that if she did he would prove that he truly didn't think she was worth the effort. And then she would have to know, not just suspect deep down that there was nothing about her that grabbed hold of anyone tight enough to incite change.

Her father had been so lost in his grief over his wife that he had not been able to pull out of it for the sake of his daughter. Leon, on the other hand, had drawn him out in a way she never had. Perhaps it was their matching grief. She could easily see that now. At the time, she hadn't realized the loss that Leon was contending with.

Still, at the time it seemed very much like there was something missing in her that other people seemed to possess. A spark that she just couldn't seem to ignite inside of herself.

And now, she had finally tried. She had finally demanded the impossible.

He hadn't been able to give it. Not to her.

She lifted her head, raising her face toward the sky, not caring as the droplets landed on her skin, rolling down her face. She could feel something expanding inside her chest—anger, desperation. She could feel herself expanding, changing. Perhaps because she was out here alone. Perhaps because she was no longer trying to shrink herself, contort herself to fit someone else's view of who she was.

It was so easy for her to imagine she wasn't worth it. That she didn't have what it took to inspire passion in someone. But who knew her? Did anyone? She had spent so long being quiet. Not making demands. How would anyone know what she wanted? How would anyone know that she was worth it?

She had never once behaved as though she was worth it. She had hidden herself away, made herself quiet. Made herself pale. And it had been easy, earlier in the rose garden when Leon was looking at her, when he was kissing her, to imagine that she could be loud. In that space, with his permission. But it was much harder when he had been looking at her with cold, dispassionate eyes. When he wished she would shrink again, and not ask quite so much. That had been the true test.

The test of whether or not she had the strength to be heard. Whether or not she could stand her ground and ask for these things when someone else said they didn't want to give them.

She realized finally that even if Leon didn't think she was worth it, even if her father had never thought she was worth it...*she* thought she was.

She realized it with a rush of absolute certainty and strength. How could she be a mother to Isabella if she taught her that a woman should twist and contort and bend endlessly in order to accommodate other people in her life?

She didn't want that little girl to bend, not even once. The world should bend around her, because she had value that was beyond estimation.

But Rose would never be able to teach her that if she didn't live her own life in that way.

So she got up off the ground.

She spread her arms wide, still facing the heavens, water cascading down her body. Her dress was soaked, probably ruined. Her marriage was ruined.

Her life was not.

Her life would be what she made it. She wanted love. She deserved love. She did not deserve to tiptoe around musty halls hoping for attention. She did not deserve to spend her entire professional life continuing to pour into her father's legacy. She deserved to create her own.

She did not deserve to have her love defined by Leon. To have him put limitations on it. Because she deserved to give it to someone who loved her back.

God knew, he would probably always have her love. That was the simple truth. She had loved Leon Carides from the moment she had first seen him and she very seriously doubted that that would change. But the way she responded to it had to.

Her only real concern was how this would affect her relationship with Isabella. She truly had grown to love the baby as her own. But then, Leon *did* love his daughter. And he wanted her to have a mother. They could come to an agreement, on that she was confident.

But she would have to leave this house behind. This thing she had been clinging to for so many years. This place that had held memories and dreams that she had so longed to live over and over again.

Tonight she had lived a dream. A fantasy. She had attended one of those beautiful parties in this wonderful home, but it hadn't fixed anything.

It was surreal, standing there, living out a scene you had always desired to be a part of, then realizing that there were no answers to be found. There were only more questions. It hadn't magically brought her happiness. Because love had still been missing. And so it hadn't mattered.

In the end, the only answer she had truly received was that it was time to grow up. It was time to stop living in the past. It was time to stop wishing that old fantasies would become a new reality.

It was time to move forward, knowing that she deserved it.

Whether or not Leon ever believed it.

She believed it. And that was all that mattered.

CHAPTER THIRTEEN

IF THERE WAS one thing Leon Carides was well acquainted with it was grief.

It was a truth about himself he was certain of as he sat on his bedroom floor, his back pressed against the wall, staring into the darkness. This feeling was old. It was familiar. A yawning cavern that was desperate to be filled.

And fill it he had done, for years. With alcohol, with sex. With work.

But here he was, sober, desiring no woman besides the one who had left him, with no choice but to allow grief to roll over him in waves. That experience was new.

It didn't take a genius to figure out why he had spent so many years avoiding the emotion. It was desolate and raw. It forced him to examine every dark space inside of him and acknowledge the fact that in many ways he was severely lacking.

Yes, he had defied the odds. Defeating poverty, climbing up the ranks in business… But it was empty. In the end, all of it was empty. What had it accomplished? What had it done for him?

All of that money and he had not been able to buy himself a soul. He had not been able to banish fear.

He had been so afraid that he had denied the existence of his own child.

He stood up suddenly, ignoring the rush of blood that made his head swim. He walked to his bedroom door, slowly making his way into the hall. Terror, his old friend, gripped his chest as he walked down the hall toward his sleeping daughter's room. Memories from the past mingling with the present as they often did in this situation.

He pushed open the door to the nursery and walked inside, fear and love wrapping itself around his heart in equal measure. He put his hand on Isabella's little back, breathing out a long, slow sigh of relief as he felt her warmth beneath his palm. As he felt her small heart beating, her back rising and falling with each indrawn breath.

He could have wept with relief. Every time.

And suddenly, a barrage of images flashed through his mind. But they weren't memories. They were visions of the future. Of Isabella growing up. Walking, going to school, dating. Driving. Going away to university.

The thousands of ways he would never be able to protect her. He would never be free of this terror that resided in his chest. Not where she was concerned. She was too precious to him. And the world around them was too uncertain.

Love would always carry this terrible weight.

He reached down and picked up his sleeping child, cradling her closely to his chest. She made a small, squeaking sound as she nuzzled deeper into him. He placed his hand over the back of her head, relishing the feel of her softness, the sweet scent that was unique to new life. He had never thought he would have this again. He hadn't wanted it.

The cost of it. There was no way to calculate it. It could tear you apart in a thousand different ways. With worry, with grief, with loss.

But this moment… In this moment he thought it might be worth all of it.

Something so valuable would never be free. It would never be without cost or risk.

He sat down in the rocking chair in the corner of the nursery, something he had not done with Isabella before. He had done it with his son, all those years ago. Sat and rocked him endlessly, singing songs that were probably inappropriate because he hadn't known any lullabies. Because he had been a seventeen-year-old father.

A small smile tipped his lips up as he began to rock Isabella.

Such a beautiful soul his son had been. He never let himself think of him. He'd buried this. This grief. This love.

But he knew for certain that if he never allowed himself to feel pain, he would never experience anything true. The past sixteen years of his life were a testament to that. The buzz from drinks faded, the pleasure from meaningless sex lasted only a few moments. None of it was real. It was all too *easy*.

The real things, the true things…they were quiet. They were darkened nurseries, sleepless nights. Vows that bound you to another person for life. They were simple. They were hard.

Babies, and beautiful women with blue eyes.

They were the impossible things.

And the most important.

It had been so easy to coast through life, as long as he wasn't allowing himself to remember what it was to feel. Ironically, he had to lose all of his memories to feel. To remember what it was to feel.

He had to get past the lies so that he could experience something true.

He had told Rose he was hollow inside. He had told himself the same. That he couldn't love her. He had told himself that from the moment he had begun to see her as a woman. He had prevented himself from touching her because he knew that once he did she would touch him, deeper than he ever wanted anyone to go. That she would reach down deep, all the way to his scarred soul and try to force him to feel again.

He knew what love was. That was the problem. He also knew what it cost.

But now he was sitting here, having lost Rose. Having hurt her. It didn't matter if he had intended to avoid feeling things for her… It was too late. He had felt things for her from the moment he'd taken her into his arms on the night of her prom.

And that was why when he had run from her, he had run so hard.

He was still running. All these years later.

"I think it's time to stop."

Leon had established a meeting with her so that they could discuss custody. She hadn't seen him for a week. She hadn't seen Isabella, either, and the loss of both of them ate at her like a vicious beast.

She was miserable. This bid for independence, for self-worth, had a high cost. And she was still on the fence about whether or not it would be worth it in the end.

As she walked into the manor, a wave of sadness washed over her. But it wasn't memories of her childhood that made her ache for this place. It was memories of her time with Leon. Of her time with Isabella.

The family she wanted to make, the real family, not a fantasy or a vague dream. The family she could have if she was just willing to take something less than love.

But if she took something less now, then she would always take something less. She had proved that for the past twenty-three years.

She blinked, continuing on up the stairs, and to Leon's office. This was like submitting to torture. But for Isabella, it was worth it.

When she walked in, Leon was sitting behind the desk. She just stood there, staring at him for a long moment. As if somehow looking at him now could get her through the rest of her life.

The sad thing was, she would see him again. She would see him hundreds of times. Thousands of times. But she wouldn't touch him. She wouldn't have him. Isabella bonded them together. Prevented her from walking away completely.

She looked away from him. "All right. I hope that we can see to all this as civilly as possible."

"Why would you have concerns about my civility?"

"Maybe it's mine that I'm worried about," she said.

"You have always been perfectly civil."

She looked back at him. "Yes. And I'm through with that. I'm tired of blending into the wood paneling of this old estate. I'm tired of trying to be accommodating to you. Just as I was accommodating to my father. I'm tired of waiting around for things to happen simply because I'm so quiet. Because I'm so good."

"You aren't quiet or good at all," he said, his voice frayed. "If you were you would still be here with me."

"Yes. Warming your bed as you saw fit and getting out of your way when you decided you wanted to warm someone else's."

"When did I ever say I wouldn't be faithful to you? You were the one who decided you couldn't believe me." He cleared his throat. "But that is not what we're here to discuss."

"We're here to discuss custody," she said, swallowing hard.

"No," he said. "I lied. I asked you to come here because I wanted to give you something."

She blinked rapidly. "What?"

"Only everything." He pushed a stack of papers over the desk toward her, then stood. "The house. The company. Everything. It's yours. There are no conditions. You love this house. And the company should always have been yours."

"But you can't... Our marriage means it's yours. I left you, which means I'm the one who forfeits it."

He shook his head. "Your father told me to take care of you. And I failed at every opportunity. At every turn. I told myself I was protecting you by staying away from you, when I was, in fact, protecting myself. Ensuring I could have everything I wanted at no cost to me."

"But..."

"This is your home. Your history. Your legacy. I never want you to feel as though you have to be with me to have it. I never want you to feel as though I kept on taking from you. Not after what I took already. Though... Rose, I swear I will be faithful to you. If you would have me."

"No," she said, taking a step back. "I can't. I can't put myself through it."

"I am giving you everything! And my word. Why do you not believe me?"

"It wasn't about believing you. It was about believing in myself. What would you say if Isabella wanted to marry a man who didn't love her?"

He looked as though he had been punched in the face. "I would tell her to stay far away from any man who didn't see her as the treasure that she is."

"And you would ask me to take less?"

"Yes. I would have. Not because I think you deserve less, Rose. But because I wanted you. I wanted you and I didn't want to have to give everything to have you. From the very beginning."

"What are you talking about?"

"I told you that when we danced together the night of your prom I wanted you. But what I didn't tell you was how much deeper it went. Because I didn't want to acknowledge it to myself. I didn't want to admit it."

"What are you saying exactly?"

"I'm a coward. I told you I didn't know how to love. I wished that I didn't. For so many years I wished that I didn't." He swallowed hard, his Adam's apple bobbing up and down. "I did. I could see it in your eyes, every time I looked at you. And… Dear God, Rose, you have no idea how much I wanted to reach out and claim that. To claim you."

He hadn't moved. He was still standing behind his desk, the large expanse of furniture between them. And she was still standing there, frozen, unable to take the chance. Unable to make the move. For fear of rejection.

Just *rejection*. She had been running scared for so long for fear of something that wasn't even fatal.

She looked at Leon, and she understood. For the very first time, she understood. It wasn't rejection he feared. It was loss. Loss he had experienced on such a keen, deep level. He had lived his entire life in avoidance of feeling that kind of pain ever again.

"And then I thought… Rose, I thought that if I married you, perhaps I could put my feelings for you in a separate compartment. Perhaps I could have you without truly having you. Without being changed by you. That was why I didn't come to you on our wedding night. Because I figured out very quickly that could not be. When I kissed you, the world turned upside down. It inverted beneath my feet, and I knew that if I were to ever put my hands on you, if I were ever to join my body to yours I would never be the same. And I had been…I had been changed by love already. I have been broken by it."

"I know," she said, her tone hushed.

"No. I don't think you do. I don't think you really understand what I'm trying to say. Because I didn't truly understand it. I had to be reduced to nothing so that I could understand exactly what I was. So I could understand what I was running from. When everything was removed, there was nothing but the truth. There was nothing but you. And I...I loved you easily. When there was no past... It was so simple to love you."

Her throat tightened, her chest feeling like a heavy weight was settled over the top of it. "Please don't. Please don't torment me with this. With the fact that you loved me when you didn't remember—"

"I'm not trying to torment you. I want you to know the truth. All these years... All this time... It was the broken things that kept me from you. It was the damage in my soul. But there was one part of me that recognized you from that first moment. That recognized you were my truth. That you were life. But I ran from it. Because I was afraid of what it would do to me to want again. To hope again. To love again. And when

I woke up in that hospital bed I didn't have fear. I had you. And I was free to have you."

"But now you remember again. So all of it was for nothing."

He slammed his hand down on the top of his desk, knocking over an hourglass, the glass clattering against the wood. "No. It was for *everything*. Because before, I had kept myself protected. Before, I had prevented myself from touching you out of a sense of self-preservation. So while I had the fantasy of what it might be like to have you, I didn't have the knowledge. But I have it now. When all of the fear was removed I claimed you. And I can't forget that." He put his fingertips on the side of the hourglass, turning it back onto its end. "I think I forgot myself sixteen years ago, not two months ago. I lost myself in grief." He looked up at her. "I do not want to forget again. I do not want my destruction to be the legacy of my son who I love so very much. I do not want the man I have been to be my legacy."

She struggled to take a breath, struggled not to hope. "It doesn't have to be."

"I will always be afraid. I will always be afraid

of losing you. I will always be afraid of the dangers that lurk around every corner when it comes to Isabella. Because that's what it is to love. But it's only a small part. Loss is only great when love is great, and I had allowed myself to forget how truly great love was. I would not even allow myself to remember Michael with any sense of joy. It is difficult. It is difficult to remember something you lost. But he was beautiful. And I should remember him that way. I should remember my time with him that way."

"Leon… There is no right way to deal with such a thing."

"There are wrong ways. Marrying a woman, wishing to possess her without actually caring for her, betraying her… Betraying your marriage vows, that's the wrong way. I have been such a coward," he repeated. "And you… You were brave. You stood out there in the rain and you demanded more for both of us. I was the one who could not give that to you. But I asked you to come here today not to discuss custody, and not even to sign over the house and Tanner Investments."

"Really?" The word was soft, strangled.

"I asked you to come here today because I needed to ask the impossible of you one more time."

Hope, joy and pain washed over her in equal measure. "It doesn't hurt to ask."

"I am a man with nothing. Being with me will give you nothing. The house is yours. The company is yours. I have nothing to offer you but myself, and it is a sorry offering indeed. This place is yours. You could have me thrown out for trespassing, erase my name from the door at Tanner Investments as though I were never there. The power is yours. But I need to ask this. Please forgive me. Please give me a second chance."

She swallowed hard, using every ounce of her strength not to launch herself over the desk and throw herself into his arms. "Why? Why should I give you a second chance now?" She was trembling. Inside and out. "The house, the company. None of that means a damn thing, you foolish man. I was ready to leave it all. I don't want it. The only thing that matters is your heart. Are you prepared to give the impossible back to me?"

He rounded the desk, moving to stand in front

of her, taking her hand in his, his dark eyes blazing into hers. "No," he said, "no, I'm not."

Her heart sank down into her stomach. "Oh."

"Because loving you was *never* impossible. And you should never have felt as though it was."

A rush of breath escaped her lips. "I'm sorry, you're going to have to be a little bit more explicit."

"I love you, Rose. When everything inside of me was a lie, you were the truth. When I knew nothing, I knew you. When I lost touch with everything, with the man I was, the man I wanted to be, you brought me back home. I loved you, but I was afraid to embrace you. And I love you now, without fear. Without reservation."

She was trembling. Shaking from her core. She could scarcely breathe, scarcely speak. But one thing was certain. No matter the pain they had endured together, no matter who owned the house, no matter how she'd been hurt by his rejection...

Her love for him remained.

"Tell me more," she said.

"I love you," he ground out. "And I am terrified to my soul over it. It is why I ran from you, so far and so fast. It's why I'm giving you all of these things…my possessions, because I feel too unequal, too empty to offer only myself. I am a sinner, Rose. Some would say beyond redemption. Perhaps they are correct. Perhaps I have no right to ask for love, not after what I've done. But I am. Because I have to. As certainly as I have to breathe to live, I have to love you. And beg for your love in return."

A tear slid down her cheek, the clouds parting in her soul and allowing a shaft of light to shine through.

Hope.

It was brighter than fear. Brighter than anger. Stronger than pain. It flooded her, warmed her. And she knew that this was the moment. When she stayed safe, but wounded, hiding in the dark.

Or when she stepped into the light and embraced forgiveness. Redemption. Love.

There was no question. Because all she had ever wanted was there, in the light. And all she had to do was reach out and take him.

"Oh, Leon, I love you, too." She wrapped her arms around his neck, kissing him on the cheek, the jaw, the corner of his mouth. "I really do."

"Why do you love me?" he asked, the words raw and tortured.

She traced his features with her fingertips, memorized his face. "That is the hardest and easiest question. Sometimes I think my love for you simply walked in right along with you, that very first day you came to Tanner house. That in that moment it lodged itself in me, and I have never been free of it since. But it's more than that. Deeper. You always saw me. Who I could be. Not just the small, mousy creature I felt like. And you challenged me. In a lot of ways I wish you hadn't. And in the years since, in this moment, it has become a choice. One I have made knowing you, all of you. Your perfections and your broken edges. It is more precious because of that. More real. More costly and more special than you'll ever know."

"I know you have no reason to trust me."

"That isn't true. Because for all your sins you didn't lie to me."

"Except for the marriage vows."

"Yes. That was wrong of you. Though given the circumstances…you were not given much choice but to marry me out of your loyalty to my father." She cleared her throat. "I never went and asked you for what I wanted. You know, before your accident, I was going to ask you for a divorce."

He took a step back. "You were?"

"Yes. I thought I was being brave. I thought I was moving on with my life by separating from you. But the simple fact is I was just running. I either hid, or I ran. But I certainly never asked you for what I wanted."

"Ask me," he said, his voice raw as he gathered her back into his arms. "Ask me now."

"Be my husband. In every sense of the word. Love me. Love our children, and in that I include Isabella. Be faithful to me."

"I swear it," he said. "With all of the memories of my grief, all of the memories of my sins, with the man I have been and the man I hope to be, I swear it. I will be your husband, I will forsake all others and I will do it happily. I will choose love over fear, every day. And some days I know it will have to be a choice, a very purposeful choice, but I swear to you that I will come to you when it threatens to overwhelm me."

"So will I. I'm not going to stay silent when I want something from you. I'm going to tell you."

"Good."

"I might make your life a living hell."

He cupped her cheek, skimming his thumb over her cheekbone. "The only living hell I can imagine is a life without you. I know what love costs, Rose. I know it better than most. And I choose it anyway. I choose you." He leaned in, kissing her lips lightly. "When I say that I love you it is with the knowledge of what that might cost. When I say that I love you, you can trust that it's real."

"I do," she said, her lips brushing against his as she spoke.

Rose remembered clearly being told that Leon's survival was a miracle after the accident. And it was. But here in her home—their home—safe in his embrace, she understood that survival wasn't the true miracle.

It was living.

EPILOGUE

LEON REMARRIED ROSE the following year. It was entirely different to that first wedding three years earlier. When a pale, young bride had walked toward him, unsure of what exactly she was getting herself into.

Giving herself to a man she knew didn't love her. Things had changed. He had changed.

Today, when Rose walked down the aisle toward him, it wasn't in a heavy veil that concealed her face from him. Today, she had her hair loose, with a crown of pink flowers adding a pop of brightness to her pale blonde beauty.

Her dress was simple. Long and flowing, swirling around her feet. She looked like an angel. And if anyone would have asked, he would have said that Rose Tanner was, without a doubt, his angel.

She had saved him. From his grief. From loneliness. And most especially from himself.

This time, when he took her hands in his and made vows, they were vows he had written himself. Vows that came from his heart, not from tradition. Not from anyone else.

"Rose, I made promises to you once before. But they were empty. I didn't keep them. I spoke the words, but I didn't make vows. But now... now I'm making vows. You're the reason my heart beats. You're the reason I live. The reason I love. I promise you my life. I promise my love and my fidelity. I know there is no happiness for me outside of this, outside of us. I spent years taking you for granted. I spent years squandering what we could have had. I was given a precious gift, and I was far too lost to truly appreciate it." He tightened his hold on her hands. "But now I know. I have seen death, Rose. And I have lived it. A sort of survival that isn't living at all, just breathing. But you...you are life. My life. My breath. My truth."

When they had finished speaking their vows, Rose turned and took Isabella from the arms of her maid of honor, holding the little girl—who was growing far too quickly for Leon's taste—close. "I promise to love you, too," she whispered. "We're a family."

Leon took hold of his daughter's hand. "You both have me. My heart. Always."

Later, there was cake, and there was dancing. And a very cranky Isabella had to be taken back to the house by the nanny.

But Leon and Rose stayed, until the very last song. He held her tightly against him, letting the music wrap itself around them.

The whole world, all of the people, the past and everyone in it, fell away.

And all he could see were Rose's blue eyes.

* * * * *

If you enjoyed this story,
don't miss the start of Maisey Yates's
fabulous new trilogy;
HEIRS BEFORE VOWS…
THE SPANIARD'S PREGNANT BRIDE
Available February 2017

And look out for
THE PRINCE'S PREGNANT MISTRESS
And
THE ITALIAN'S PREGNANT VIRGIN
Coming soon!

MILLS & BOON®
Large Print – December 2016

The Di Sione Secret Baby
Maya Blake

Carides's Forgotten Wife
Maisey Yates

The Playboy's Ruthless Pursuit
Miranda Lee

His Mistress for a Week
Melanie Milburne

Crowned for the Prince's Heir
Sharon Kendrick

In the Sheikh's Service
Susan Stephens

Marrying Her Royal Enemy
Jennifer Hayward

An Unlikely Bride for the Billionaire
Michelle Douglas

Falling for the Secret Millionaire
Kate Hardy

The Forbidden Prince
Alison Roberts

The Best Man's Guarded Heart
Katrina Cudmore

MILLS & BOON®
Large Print – January 2017

To Blackmail a Di Sione
Rachael Thomas

A Ring for Vincenzo's Heir
Jennie Lucas

Demetriou Demands His Child
Kate Hewitt

Trapped by Vialli's Vows
Chantelle Shaw

The Sheikh's Baby Scandal
Carol Marinelli

Defying the Billionaire's Command
Michelle Conder

The Secret Beneath the Veil
Dani Collins

Stepping into the Prince's World
Marion Lennox

Unveiling the Bridesmaid
Jessica Gilmore

The CEO's Surprise Family
Teresa Carpenter

The Billionaire from Her Past
Leah Ashton

MILLS & BOON®

Why shop at millsandboon.co.uk?

Each year, thousands of romance readers find their perfect read at millsandboon.co.uk. That's because we're passionate about bringing you the very best romantic fiction. Here are some of the advantages of shopping at www.millsandboon.co.uk:

* **Get new books first**—you'll be able to buy your favourite books one month before they hit the shops

* **Get exclusive discounts**—you'll also be able to buy our specially created monthly collections, with up to 50% off the RRP

* **Find your favourite authors**—latest news, interviews and new releases for all your favourite authors and series on our website, plus ideas for what to try next

* **Join in**—once you've bought your favourite books, don't forget to register with us to rate, review and join in the discussions

Visit **www.millsandboon.co.uk**
for all this and more today!